DREAMWORLD
TALES FROM THE SUBCONSCIOUS

Cozzen Publications
Claremont, N.C. 28610

R. Duane Cozzen is also the author of

Live Radio - *A Humerous and Serious Look At Small Market Radio*

ISBN: 978-0-6151-4126-8

Printed in United States of America by Lulu Industries, Raleigh, NC
Published by Cozzen Publications, Claremont, NC

Front cover design copyright © 2010: *Mandy Buff / mandybuff.com*
Editing: *Sabrina Valles / valles.sabrina@yahoo.com*
Back cover photo copyright © 2010: *Mona Acker Cozzen Photography*

DREAMWORLD
TALES FROM THE SUBCONSCIOUS

by

R. Duane Cozzen

DEDICATION

TO MY LOVING WIFE, MONA ACKER COZZEN, WHO GAVE ME THE IDEA FOR ZOONOSIS AND INSPIRED ME TO WRITE WHY ME!? AND OVERLY PROTECTIVE FROM ACTUAL DREAMS SHE HAD. ALSO TO THE KIDS: CASSIE, BRIANNA, AND ROGER.

IN LOVING MEMORY OF:

CHRISTOPHER AARON ACKER

TABLE OF CONTENTS

INTRODUCTION

I AM A COLLECTOR OF DREAMS - THOSE NIGHTLY IMAGES THAT ENTER OUR WORLD FROM THE SUBCONSCIOUS.

WHEN WE FALL INTO THE ABYSS OF SLEEP, OUR MIND SURRENDERS TO AN UNKNOWN WORLD OF PHANTASMAGORIA WHERE THOUGHTS AND IMAGES, FROM THAT MYSTERIOUS PART OF OUR BRAIN, ARE SET FREE TO INTERTWINE INTO A TALE OF ILLUSION. OR IS IT ILLUSION?

DURING THIS SLUMBER TIME, FICTION AND REALITY ARE ORCHESTRATED TO CREATE A PLAY THAT IS DIRECTED BY OUR SUBCONSCIOUS, EDITED BY OUR IMAGINATION, AND PRODUCED BY OUR INNERMOST FEELINGS AND THOUGHTS.

MANY OF THESE NIGHTLY SOJOURNS WE WOULD LIKE TO REMEMBER, FOR THEY BRING BACK PLEASANT TOUCHES, SMELLS, TASTES AND FEELINGS. SOMETIMES OUR PEACEFUL SLUMBER IS INVADED BY HORRENDOUS BEINGS AND EVENTS THAT CAN CAUSE THE BRAVEST SOUL TO AWAKEN IN A STATE OF PANIC. THAT'S WHEN THE DREAMWORLD BECOMES A NIGHTMARE. IT'S PURPOSE? PLAY HAVOC WITH OUR MINDS!

IN THE PAGES THAT FOLLOW, YOU WILL FIND SOME OF MY FAVORITE FANTASIES-OF-THE-NIGHT. SOME ARE HARMLESS, AND SOME ARE FROM THE DARK SHADOWS OF THE DREAM-WORLD.

THIS IS A COLLECTION FROM THE SUBCONSCIOUS, WHERE REALITY BECOMES ILLUSION, AND ILLUSION BECOMES REALITY.

WELCOME TO MY...DREAMWORLD.

A Strange Night

You may think I'm crazy! I thought so myself at first, but I have it on video, proof that that night was indeed, a strange night!

It began with a full moon. Not that I'm superstitious, not the least bit, but the moon *was full* – I'll leave it at that. It was a quiet night too; the wind calm, the sky clear, even the crickets and other insects of the night seemed to be mute.

I had just finished my microwaved supper of meatloaf, mashed potatoes and peas, and had settled down into my favorite chair in the den to read, when I heard a strange rumbling sound. At first, I thought it was the sound of a passing car or truck; but the more I listened, the more apparent it became that the sound was coming from within my own home. Half raising myself up from my chair to hear better, I realized that it was something rolling across the hardwood floor. Then–*I saw it!*

The upright vacuum cleaner rolled past the doorway of the den, stopping just out of sight. Thinking it had miraculously rolled out of its resting place from the hall closet, I went to retrieve it. Before I could reach the doorway, I heard the rumbling again and was horrified when the vacuum cleaner backed into the doorway, stopped, and rolled into the den; coming to rest just inches in front of me.

Mind you, it wasn't plugged in, and I can assure you the floors in my house are as level as can be. The machine then rolled around me to the center of the room, spun on its rear wheels, and then back to the doorway, where it stopped again.

Now, I'm not a man of weak character, and God forbid that I be influenced by drug or drink, but as sure as I'm writing this, the vacuum cleaner turned to me and bowed, before proceeding down the hallway.

Being a curious person by nature, I immediately followed it into the living room where I found it standing upright in the middle of the floor. As I stepped into the room, it bowed to me – _again_. I was then startled by a loud racket coming from the kitchen.

Turning my attention away from the still-bowing vacuum cleaner, I was befuddled when I saw the ironing board come through the kitchen door on all fours, humping like a caterpillar. It stopped in front of me, stood up and took a bow.

Turning my attention from the ironing board back to the vacuum cleaner, which had finally ceased its bowing, I found myself in a confused state of mind.

Then, to my _amazement_, the lamp jumped off the end table onto the couch, and began jumping up and down. The couch, not to be outdone by the wayward lamp, began moving from side-to-side in a sort-of dance. The telephone was sliding, playfully, from one end of the end table to the other. It was like watching an old "Mickey Mouse" cartoon.

I, to say the least, was in awe to see such strange happenings in my own house.

If only you could have seen me! What a sight I must have been to look at - mouth wide open, eyes as wide as saucers, hands on the top of my head!

Without warning, I was pushed aside from my vantage point by the broom and mop, as they made *their* way into the living room. Once inside, they began to dance a waltz. A few pots and pans from the kitchen paraded by me in single file, each moving in their own peculiar way.

In the center of the room, the coffee table stood on two legs and began walking back and forth from one end of the room to the other; it was joined by another end table.

I rubbed my eyes hoping that everything would return to normal when I opened them again, but when I did – *it got worse*! The living room curtains were now joining in on the festivities, fluttering in the air, while on the floor the throw rug began doing a snake-like dance.

Transfixed by what was happening before me, I tried in vain to make some sense of it all. Then, I remembered the video-recorder. Hurriedly, I went back to the den to retrieve it. When I had returned, more articles of the house had joined in, including six pairs of knives and forks, which were dancing animatedly on the floor.

As I began filming, each item seemed to be showing off for the camera trying to out-do each other. The commotion went on for about thirty-minutes when, one-by-one, each returned to its original resting place. Soon, the room was back to normal and I turned off the video-recorder.

11. - *A Strange Night*

This happened last week and I have since sent the videotape to a local television station. This could be the *biggest* story of the year, defying every physics law known to man.

I must have made a very big impression because some official-looking people came to my home yesterday. They said they had a nice place for me to stay. I guess, since this is such a *big* discovery, they need to keep me in a secure place. It's not bad. I've got all the food I can eat and my own private nurse and doctor.

The only thing I don't like about it are the bars on the windows. Oh well, you can never be *too* safe.

I've got to go now – I think I just heard the lamp run into the bathroom.

THE STORM

What you are about to read is a true account of an incident that happened to me during a very lonely and desolate time in my life. A time, when all that mattered to me was obtaining notoriety as a published writer.

In my endless quest for such, I found myself traveling to various publishing houses across this great country of ours, submitting my works in person. I wasn't a patient man then, and sending manuscripts by mail, or even email, took too long to get a response. If I were to be rejected, I wanted to be told in person, not by receiving a rejection letter or email. So I traveled, staying in various cities, waiting for a "yes" or "no" answer. These expeditions left very little time for family and friends, filling me with a bitterness I couldn't shake.

On one of these sojourns, I found myself lost on a small country road about twenty miles north of Richmond, Virginia. As my mode of transportation had developed internal problems, I was left with no other choice but to find civilization on foot; just as a summer's evening storm began approaching from the West.

Leaving my poor excuse for a car to fend for itself, I began walking down the dusty dirt road. I had progressed about a mile, when an eerie feeling of being watched came over me. Looking over my left shoulder I saw nothing, only the deserted road. Then, I heard the distinct call of a raven, sending a cold chill up and down my spine.

Being a writer, I attributed this to my over-active imagination and continued my quest to find civilization.

Looking up at the sky, I observed large gray and black clouds forming monstrous shapes. The wind was increasing and the trees, bordering each side of the road, began to sway back and forth.

It was getting darker, and the combination of the wind and tree movement sent my imagination racing. At times, I thought I saw someone standing in the middle of the road before me, and that nagging sensation of being watched increased. Then, there it was again – *the call of a raven.*

As the storm grew in size, I quickened my pace. With each step I took, my heart began to beat faster and faster. Lightening played in the dark clouds above, as the low rumbling sound of thunder reached my ears. When the first drops of rain began to fall, they would hit the dirt road creating small puffs of dust. It wouldn't be long before the sporadic rain drops would intensify, leaving me soaked to the bone.

Finding some sort of shelter, to wait out the storm, became my first priority. As I looked ahead of me, the road now turning to mud as the rain hit it with a vengeance, seemed to lead into a black abyss.

I searched in vain for any signs of suitable cover and had almost given up, when a flash of lightening outlined a dilapidated shack standing about twenty feet off the roadway to my left.

While fighting my way through the underbrush, the sensation of being watched enveloped my inner soul. Even as the storm's wind and thunder began to crescendo, I could hear that nagging cry of the raven

Finally, I reached the door to the shack, and opened it with such force that I landed on the dusty wooden floor.

When I had regained my faculties, I closed the door and looked around, waiting for my eyes to adjust to the darkness. In the dim light, I was able to make out a small window to the left of the door. Taking a lighter out of my pocket, and after several attempts to get it to ignite, I was finally able to produce a small flame, barely illuminating the shapes of a wooden table upon which a half-spent candle sat. Two ladder-back chairs lay precariously on the floor near the table. In one corner were the remnants of an old wood burning stove.

After lighting the candle, I up-righted the chairs, taking the sturdier one for myself, pushing it up to the table and prepared to wait out the storm.

I had just begun to regain my breath from the vigorous dash through the brush, when there was a sudden blinding flash of lightening, followed by an ear-piercing burst of thunder. So intense was it, that the shack vibrated, almost knocking me out of my chair.

Then, as if on cue, the door flew open, crashing into the back of the wall. Illuminated by the flashes of lightening stood the figure of a small man in the doorway. The nagging call of the raven could be heard just outside.

Without saying a word, the man walked to the table, sat down in the vacant chair across from me, laying both arms on the tables top placing the right hand over the left, as the door slowly closed mysteriously behind him.

My candle had been extinguished with the opening of the door so I nervously ignited it again. From the faint glow I could make out the man's features. He appeared to be about five feet tall, and though he was small in stature, his frame was athletic looking.

His face had the pale complexion of an angel. He had a weak chin and a small mouth which sported a dark mustache. His eyes were gray and intense. His forehead was large, and his dark disarrayed hair matched the dark clothing he wore.

I was about to ask the man his name, but he held his hand up to silence me. He began to speak in a gentle, haunting voice, that made the hairs on the back of my neck stand straight up. What he was about to divulge would change my life – *forever!*

"I am a man doomed to this earth," he began, looking down at the table. After a short pause he raised his eyes, looked into mine, and continued his narrative, "I, like you, am lonely in heart and soul. I, too, was a writer who has experienced success and failure, riches and poverty. I have loved and been loved—I have hated and been hated."

When he paused again, I noticed a tear rolling down his left cheek. As he resumed his narrative, his words were more profound. "I longed to be famous; driven to do insane deeds; the worst, my addiction to spirits. This drinking caused me endless nights of illness and heart-ache, not only for me, but for my true love."

With saddened eyes he continued, "Drugs too, have also played a disastrous role in my life—thinking they were a source of creativity. Though I eventually gained the notoriety I had hoped for, I remained a poor man 'til the end."

As he talked, I began to see bits and pieces of my own life unfolding before me. I, too, had taken to drink in times of inactivity. I felt the anguish and heartache of hurting those I truly loved.

He continued to speak, but I did not hear the words. It was as though I knew what he was saying without hearing him. When the words stopped, my eyes were full of tears, as were his. He had touched my inner soul. Then, as if an unknown force were calling to him, he rose to his feet, turned, and with his head bent down, slowly walked toward the door.

"Please wait," I begged. "You have changed my life. Please tell me your name."

Stopping in the doorway, he slowly turned and said, "Some called me–*Israfel*". Then he vanished, leaving me dumbfounded, but a better man.

The storm had passed during the course of his narrative. I blew out the candle, and put my lighter into my coat pocket. As I stepped out under the clear evening sky, I heard the faint call of the raven.

Continuing my journey, the name *Israfel* kept going through my mind. I had heard the name before, but where? Then it hit me! It was the childhood name of...*Edgar Allen Poe*. The more I walked, the lighter my footsteps became. There was also a lightness in my heart.

"Thank you, *Israfel*," I said, subtly to myself.

THE CAVE

THE LAST STAND OF COMMANDER LAZE

The cave wasn't too uncomfortable. Actually, it was rather nice for a cave. The entrance was elevated high enough to prevent the little devils from getting to him. Inside, there were two smaller caverns. One he used as sleeping quarters, the other a work area. The latter is where Commander Robert Laze spent most of his time. Here is where he devised ways to defend himself. This he had done successfully for the past twelve months, but now, they were getting wise to his little devices of war.

At first his booby traps, using a few bits of cord and thermogrenades he had salvaged from the ship, were sufficient. These he had buried in the flowing sand, but after the little black devils had stumbled onto a dozen or so, they learned to move more cautiously.

Laze then developed the flying buzz bomb, using small anti-gravity cargo movers with thermogrenades carefully placed on top. He was able to control these remotely; by pressing a button, the disc would turn over, dropping the grenade on top of its target.

Unfortunately for Laze, the creatures soon realized that the soft buzzing sound of the anti-gravity cargo movers meant death, scattering them to immediately seek shelter. At least these devices of war were keeping them at bay – *for now.*

A year ago, in Solar Year 79, Commander Laze and a crew of five had crashed-landed on the desert planet; Laze, the only survivor. Their five year mission was to explore a newly discovered planet in the Zarius sector. They were nearing the Zarius sector, when a problem developed in the navigational computer putting them in uncharted space. They roamed aimlessly for two months, until their long range scanner picked up the desert planet.

Though it was mostly desert, there were small mountains rising above the sand, about one-to-two miles apart. Each mountain was two-hundred to five-hundred feet high. The scanners also showed fresh water around the mountains with vegetation covering about sixty percent of the surface. One odd feature was that the sand moved slowly up and down, like an ocean, but the scanners could not perforate the sand enough to learn why.

They were two days from the planet when another problem developed; this time in the propulsion system. Laze, reluctantly, gave the order to try for a crash landing. He was hoping the sand would cushion the impact, but it was more than he bargained for. When the craft hit the sand, it hit hard, instantly breaking apart. All were killed, except for Laze. He had awakened from unconsciousness to find the other crew members' lifeless bodies scattered on the desert sand. Except for a small concussion and a few bruises, he was okay.

After regaining his senses, the years of training kicked in and Laze began to salvage what he could from the wreckage: food, medical supplies, weapons, tools and clothing. He carefully placed these items into categorized piles. Then he had the dreaded task of burying his shipmates, one by one, in the flowing sand. It took a little over two hours before the last had been laid to rest. He could now begin his search for suitable shelter.

About a quarter of a mile to the west, he spotted a small cave entrance halfway up a small mountain. As he climbed, he came across diminutive trees bearing a red pear shaped fruit. He picked one and put it in his pocket to be tested later. After a thirty minute struggle, Laze finally reached the cave entrance. Turning on his portable light, he stepped inside.

The cave was cool, about fifty feet in diameter, with a smaller compartment to the left. There was also a five foot in diameter pit full of water in the middle of the main section of the cave. After a quick chemical test, the water proved to be fresh and drinkable. He also cut off a small piece of the fruit and ran it through his portable food analyzer; it, too, was good for human consumption. At least he had found shelter, drinking water, and a source of fresh food.

It took Laze a day and a half to transport all he could salvage from the wrecked ship into the cave. During one of his return trips to the wreckage, he thought he saw something move across the flowing sand. This, he dismissed as a shadow produced by the sands slow ocean-like movement.

A week after the crash, Commander Laze saw the first of the little scamps. He had been scanning the desert with his field glasses when the ugly creature popped up out of the sand, like a jack-in-the-box. It was black—black as coal, and stood about four feet tall. Its body was slender with long, lanky arms and legs. The creatures hands were more like claws, than hands. Its feet were webbed. The eyes were large and dark. Its skin appeared to be hairless and leathery.

Standing on the rolling sand, about fifteen feet from the crash site, it approached the spot were Laze had buried his shipmates, sticking its pudgy nose to the sand. It looked like a bloodhound trying to find a scent.

Suddenly, two more of the creatures popped up from the sand behind the first. Each made its way to where the first was stooped over, sniffing the sand's surface. As the others neared, the first, in one fluid motion, dove head first into the sand. In less than a minute it reappeared, pulling up the body of one of the dead crew members.

Again, the first creature, now joined by his two companions, stuck their noses to the sand, and after locating their targets, dove into the sand, pulling out the remaining bodies with ease.

The first creature, who seemed to be the dominate one, began ripping the uniform off one of the bodies. When it had stripped the body of all its clothing, the creature opened its large mouth, revealing long black teeth. He bent over the body, took a large bite out of it in the abdomen area, turned to the others, and nodded approval. That's when the ghastly feast began.

Laze dropped his field glasses, becoming sick to his stomach. He felt weak, collapsing against the rock wall.

A feeling of fear and hatred began to possess him. He knew that these beasts had tasted their first morsel of human flesh, and would want more. He also realized they had a keen sense of smell, and would sooner or later pick up his scent. He knew too, that this meant–WAR!

Since that horrendous day, Laze had been killing as many of the little devils as he could. He had discovered that the creatures were not physically adapted to climb the mountains, and seemed to be dormant at night. At least, he had a fighting chance. As long as there was edible vegetation on the mountain, rations from the ship, and the water hole stayed full, he believed he could survive for quite sometime.

Laze did wonder about that water hole. It never ran dry. Always full to the brim, and the water remained fresh. He recalled how the ships scanners had detected water around the mountains and assumed its source was an underground spring.

On the first anniversary of the crash landing, Laze woke with a start. He had a nightmare. The dream had consisted of the little black barbarians standing before him in the cave. He had fought furiously before being cornered at the water hole. Looking down at the water, he realized it might be his only source of escape. Better to drown than to be eaten alive by these monsters.

As he jumped into the water he had awakened, shaking and covered in sweat. When he realized that it had been a nightmare, he quickly got up from his make shift bed to begin the day's work.

Laze had survived for twelve months and today was to be a cele-bration, of sorts. He was planning the biggest ordinance display to date. He was bound and determined to give the little black devils all the fire power he could muster.

The plan was simple. Give them such a display of weaponry that it would scare them away, hopefully for good. He would be a force to reckon with. If he killed enough of them, maybe they would realize that pursuing the last bit of human flesh wasn't worth it. Maybe, just maybe, they would leave him alone – *for good.*

Using the last of his arsenal, Commander Laze had worked through most of the night, rigging up every homemade weapon he could think of. He would attack at daylight when the creatures first showed their ugly faces. First he would use the flying buzz bombs, and other homemade explosive devices, and finish up with the last of the thermogrenades. These, he had rigged on catapults around the cave's entrance. He worked feverishly, patiently, waiting for dawn.

Finally, the first rays of light pierced through the cave's entrance. Laze felt a sense of accomplishment. He would finally get revenge! Soon the little devils would appear and Laze would have his day.

SPLASH.

Laze turned toward the water hole—he saw nothing.

SPLASH.

Laze turned nervously toward the water hole again, but quickly jerked his head back. He *couldn't* be distracted, not now, not when the grand finale was about to begin.

As the sun began to rise higher he picked up his field glasses, scanning the rolling sand.

"Where are those little devils?" he asked himself threw gritted teeth.

S*PLASH, Flap, flap, flap.*

Slowly, Laze lowered the field glasses.

"No, it can't be!" he exclaimed, slowly turning his head in the direction of the water hole, just in time to see a black shadow hovering over him, holding a big stick over his head.

CRACK!

As Laze drifted into unconsciousness he mumbled, "Nooo....they live in the sand. Not the water. Not the...."

CRACK!

"You know, (*munch, munch*) you were right," said the first creature to the others. "They do taste better fresh."

"You're quite right," began the second, mouth full, smacking his lips. "It's strange though. You'd think a smart creature like this would have realized," (pausing long enough to swallow), "that there's a fresh water sea under the sand."

"Speaking of that," began the third, throwing a rib bone over his left shoulder, "I'm getting back into the water, I'll get a rash if I stay out too long."

FLAP, FLAP, FLAP...(BURP)....SPLASH.

RAILROAD HEAVEN

Sometimes, late at night, I can still hear it. The ominous sound of a steam locomotive's whistle, one long and two short blasts. A sound so distant and so very lucid. It can only be compared to the desolate sound of a lone wolf crying in the dead of night. It wasn't until a few years ago that I discovered the source of this prophetic train whistle.

Late one spring night, I had ventured out for my usual evening walk. As is my habit, I took the path towards an old abandoned railroad track. Across the tracks stood a dilapidated coal chute and sand house. About a quarter to midnight, I decided to make my way back home. Having only walked a few paces, I heard the haunting one long and two short blasts of a steam locomotive. I knew for a fact that this particular line had been abandoned for at least ten years, so that sonorous whistle sent a cold chill throughout my body.

After the second cry from the engines whistle, I turned in my tracks and began walking, once again, toward the abandoned line. I soon found myself standing by the railway bed looking in both directions for any sign of the locomotive's head light, but none could be seen.

Suddenly, there it was again. One long and two short blasts. This time it sounded closer. By now, my curiosity getting the better of me, I stepped onto the tracks for a better look.

"A man can get killed that way," said a gruff voice.

Startled, I turned toward the coal chute where I had heard the voice.

"I said, a man could get killed standing on the tracks," said the voice again.

"Who's there?" I demanded, walking toward the coal chute. "Show yourself."

"This is private property you know," grumbled the voice from the shadows.

"Sorry," I said, trying to find the owner of the voice, "I was out for a walk; heard the train whistle, so I was....."

"That would be the midnight express," interrupted the voice, "best you git yourself out of here before she arrives."

As I continued to cautiously walk toward the coal chute, I could barely make out the figure of man sitting on a wooden crate at the base of it.

"I thought this line was closed," I said candidly.

"To some, yes," he said in a melancholy voice. "To others, no."

"Care to explain?" I asked, still walking toward him.

"Will you go away if I do?" he asked.

When I promised I would, he motioned for me to sit down beside him.

As I settled onto another old wooden crate beside him, I was able to make out the mysterious man's features. He was a man of around thirty-five years, dressed in coveralls and a red plaid shirt. The skin on his face was rough and leathery looking. It was the face of a man who had spent many years working in the hot summer sun, and the cold wind of winter. His eyes were dark and haunting. His dark hair was combed straight back.

In his left hand he held a darkened red lantern. Looking at me with dark eyes, he began to tell me the story of the ghostly train whistle.

"The train you hear coming," he began, turning his head toward the tracks "ain't no ordinary train. *It's special.* My job, is to make sure that all the passengers assigned to this train get on-board. The whistle you hear, one long and two shorts, is the signal for these special passengers to prepare to board."

The stranger turned his gaze back towards me, as he continued his narrative, "This train is for engineers, conductors, brakemen, firemen, yard workers, shop workers, and all of those involved with the rail-road, past and present.

"We've worked the Alabama, Tennessee & Northern; Central of Georgia, and the Chicago North Shore & Milwaukee. Let's not forget the old Southern; the Norfolk Southern, The Great Northern Pacific Electric, Norfolk Western, the Pennsylvania Railroad System and the Southern, high balling from Norfolk, Virginia to the coastal town of Morehead City, North Carolina."

As he spoke, you could hear the steam whistle of the approaching locomotive getting louder—the one long and two shorts.

"We've carried passengers, too," he continued, once again turning his gaze toward the tracks. "Some by electric trolley from Fort Dodge to Des Moines, riding across the Fort Dodge Line's famous high bridge near Boone, Iowa. In 1892, our four wheeled steam powered New York Central Dewitt Clinton carried passengers in cars that looked like stage coaches.

My friend, we've hauled coal, cars, hobos, lettuce, tanks and soldiers—coast to coast.

"Some of us are from small lines like the Charlotte Harbor & Northern; The Alexander County Railroad, the Ann Arbor, the Tallulah Falls, and big lines like the Seaboard Coast, Penn Central, and the Old Wabash. No matter the size, we are a brotherhood of rails.

"We've traveled thousands of miles across the United States, carrying cargo and passengers with pride. For some of us, it has been our life. Many have given their lives to keep these trains moving."

He paused and looked down the track, as the haunting train whistle sounded again. It seemed to be almost upon us now.

"That, my friend, is why I'm here," he said standing up, "and why you must go."

At that instant, the coming train blew her ghostly one long and two shorts.

"Thank you," I said, getting up to leave. "I think I understand."

He didn't verbally respond, instead he lit the red lantern and walked to the edge of the railroad tracks. There he stood, lantern in hand, transfixed and looking down the tracks in the direction of the approaching train. I took my leave and headed back across the tracks to the path that had led me there. When I turned around for one last look, all I could see was the red glow of the lantern swaying back and forth. Slowly, I began to walk down the path when the commotion of a steam locomotive coming to a stop caused me turn and look. What I saw was the most beautiful train I had ever seen. The steam engine was a Baldwin Big Boy with tender, both the color of polished gold. She was pulling five white Pullman passenger cars, all trimmed in gold and silver. The whole train appeared to be illuminated in white, surrounded in a supernatural fog.

Glowing multicolored spheres of light began to fly in from every direction toward the train, each being absorbed as they entered the preternatural fog that surrounded it. The phenomena lasted less than a minute, and then the gold engine blew her whistle.

The gold bell atop the Big Boy rang, resonating throughout the night. The drive wheels slowly began to rotate, building up speed, as she slowly pulled away.

Unable to move, I stood there mesmerized by its beauty. As the last car rolled past me, she gave one final whistle—one long and two shorts—then the train vanished and all was quiet. Once again, I turned down the path toward home. As I walked, the event I had just witnessed replayed through my mind.

Opening the door to my bungalow, I looked over my left shoulder in the direction of the abandoned railroad tracks, and smiled. I had been blessed. I had been granted something no one had ever experienced. A chance to see the train, whose only destination is to....

Railroad Heaven

WHY ME!?

Aliens. They look like us and act like us, but move stiffly. I know who they are. I know they're planning to take over the world. They know what I look like. I have to run. I can't shake them. They made the bus I was going to get on explode. They didn't realize I saw one of them. Didn't get on. It was destroyed! Those poor people. Wish I could have warned them. Got to get to the airport. Got to go to Amsterdam. It's safe there. They haven't got there yet. I don't understand why no one else knows them or can tell they aren't human. Why are they after me!? Why me? WHY ME!?"

So read the note found at the missing woman's apartment.

Rayemen had only been missing for a day when her landlady called the police. It wasn't normal for Rayemen not to stop by, at least once during the day, to talk to her. It was a part of the day she enjoyed. Concerned, she had entered the apartment and found the note. That's what she told the police detective.

"I'm really worried for her," said the landlady, hands shaking as she talked to the investigator. "It's just not like her not to come by."

The note had been found laying on a desk in the missing woman's living room. The detective held it in his gloved hand, studying it. The handwriting was hurried, but neat.

"Here, bag this," the detective said softly, handing the piece of paper to an officer. "I think we'll find this one with a bullet in her head somewhere."

"You think she's mental?" asked the officer.

"I don't *think it*," replied the detective heading toward the door, "*I know it!*"

Rayemen hurried down the busy sidewalk trying not to bump into anyone and draw attention to herself. It was hard not to. Her long blonde hair and bedroom blue eyes, complimented her tall hourglass figure. Every man she came in contact with turned their gaze toward her; even the women looked in envy. She met their gaze, not to flirt, but to make sure they weren't one of them. As long as they walked normal, not stiffly, they were okay.

It's not that they walked with stiff arm and leg movements, where the elbows and knees did not bend, but more like an android. Always with perfect posture and no expression on their faces. When they spoke, their mouths moved as though their jaws were wired together. Rayemen couldn't understand why no one else could see this. Why was *she* the only one who noticed that they were different. Something wasn't right with them. She could see and sense it.

Making her way toward the airport, the events of the last few hours kept going through her mind.

She had awakened from a nightmare in a cold sweat. She couldn't remember what the dream was about, but it left her with an uneasy feeling that wouldn't go away.

While getting dressed for work, the feeling began to overwhelm her. She felt as though she were being watched. Looking out of her bedroom window, in her modest second story Washington, D.C. apartment, she could see the cars and people as they made their way to work, or some unknown destination. The siren from a fire engine could be heard in the distance, growing louder and then fading away, as it went through the corner intersection.

Looking down at the people on the sidewalk, she noticed a man across the street standing in front of a baker's shop. At first, he appeared to be a normal blue collar worker killing time, but the more she looked at him, the more leery she became of his presence there.

He was wearing gray slacks and a white shirt unbuttoned at the collar. He was unusually tall, well over seven feet and sported unnatural-looking jet-black hair. He seemed to be staring at her apartment building's front door, barely moving, standing there like a soldier who had been ordered at attention and determined to maintain that stance until ordered otherwise.

Leaving the security of her apartment building, Rayemen started walking south toward her bus stop. As she walked, she again had a feeling that someone was watching her. She wanted to turn around and look, but was afraid to. Finally, she mustered up the courage to look behind her. When she did, her eyes fell on the strange man walking about twenty feet behind her. He walked stiffly; his face expressionless. The dark eyes were fixed straight ahead, not looking at anything, or anyone in particular.

When she had walked the two blocks to her bus stop, she quickly hid in a doorway. Peeking out of her hiding place, she scanned the small crowd waiting on the bus. The strange man couldn't be found. Still feeling uneasy, Rayemen decided to stay put until the last minute before boarding her bus.

As the bus pulled up to the stop, even as the passengers began to board, she couldn't pull herself away from the doorway. Finally, she found the nerve to move, and took one step out of her hiding place. At that instant, there was a loud *boom* and the bus exploded into a ball of fire.

People were screaming—running in every direction. The impact of the explosion had knocked her off her feet and back into the doorway; slamming her body violently against the door jam. She felt a sharp pain in her right shoulder and the back of her head. Her ears were ringing, and her head was throbbing.

Rayemen ran her left hand over her right shoulder, and the back of her head. Not detecting any blood, she slowly stood up. Cautiously, she walked out onto the sidewalk, stepping on broken glass from the store front windows that had been shattered from the concussion of the blast. The crunching of glass under her feet brought her back to her senses.

Frantically, she looked into the crowd for any sign of the strange man. He was there, standing on the other side of the street, looking intently at the burning bus. Her body trembled. Had he seen her? Was he really after her? She already knew the answer to the second question. How, and why, she didn't know. She just knew. He was after her! She believed he had been responsible for the explosion. She didn't know how he did it, she just knew he did.

Get away! She's got to get away! Crouching down behind the spectators who had gathered to watch the fire department and police gain control of the scene, she began to make her way down the sidewalk. She almost passed out when a fireman grabbed her by the arm to see if she needed any assistance. Shaking her head no, she pulled away from his grip, and began to run down the sidewalk. She wanted to put as much distance between her and the stranger as she could.

Sirens from fire, rescue, and police vehicles, echoed around her. She covered her ears, trying to muffle the noise. Her head still ached, and she felt that at any moment she would collapse.

Rayemen had gone about three blocks before she found a bench to sit on. She was exhausted, confused, and felt as though her whole life was caving in on her. That uneasy feeling was still with her. It wouldn't go away. It just got worse.

"What does he want?" she asked sobbing, talking to no one. "Why is he after me? What have I done to him?!"

People passing stared at her as she cried convulsively, repeating her questions over and over again. Some almost stopped to see what was wrong, but kept walking. Many ignored her, or shook their heads in disgust thinking she was just another crack-head.

She remained on the bench until she composed herself and was able to focus on the mission at hand–to move on. Move on to where? Rayemen had no idea where she was going. Work was where she was originally headed, but she couldn't remember where she worked. She knew she had a job–*a good job*. She always had plenty of money, but where did she work? Why couldn't she remember?

She's got to get away, got to go somewhere; somewhere, away from him. If she doesn't move on, he'll find her. Come on. Get up off that bench. Get up, and walk. It doesn't matter where, just *GO!*

Amsterdam! Yes, Amsterdam. That's where she needs to go. Why Amsterdam? Where did that come from? No one had said anything to her, it just popped into her head. It's safe in Amsterdam. She knew it was safe there. She could feel it. Got to go to Amsterdam. First, she had to go back to her apartment. She needed her passport, and more money, then to the airport and the safe haven of Amsterdam!

Getting her second wind, Rayemen ran back in the direction of her apartment, carefully taking back alleys and side streets. She constantly scanned people she passed, looking for the strange man. To her relief, he wasn't to be found. She's going to make it!

Inside her apartment, she grabbed her passport from her bedroom end table and the extra cash she had hidden under her mattress. As she walked toward the door to leave, she thought of her landlady. She'll miss her. Her landlady was a sweet old woman who enjoyed her company as much as she did hers.

Got to warn her. A note. She can leave a note, warning her. Warn of what? A takeover? Some sort of takeover. That's it! They're going to takeover the world. How did she know that? Doesn't matter, she just knows. They aren't from here. They're from somewhere far off. They want to takeover the world. It's so clear now. She doesn't know why, but it is. Quickly, write her a note. At least she can warn someone.

After Rayemen finished the note, she looked out of the window onto the busy street below. Still no sign of the strange man. Maybe she had lost him. Not for long. He's searching. Still looking for her. He'll find her if she doesn't get to Amsterdam. Amsterdam is safe—*Go! Go!*

Rayemen flagged down a taxi, instructing the driver to take her to the airport. As they rode down the busy Washington streets, she continued to look at the people they passed. Still no sign of the stranger. She's going to make it. Amsterdam. It's safe there.

As the taxi pulled up in front of the airport, Rayemen handed the driver a one-hundred dollar bill and told him to keep the change. "Yes ma'am," he said, taking the bill and stuffing it in his shirt pocket, "Anytime you need a cab, *call me!*"

She didn't hear him. Got to get a ticket for the next flight to Amsterdam. The airline counter. There it is. The flight schedule. Amsterdam. When is the next flight to Amsterdam. Thirty minutes. The flight leaves in thirty minutes. Thank God. There's time. The ticket, got to get the ticket.

Rayemen quickly walked to her assigned gate, holding her ticket to Amsterdam firmly. She still had fifteen minutes to spare. She took her seat in the waiting area, anxious, nervous, and *very* scared. Amsterdam was her haven. A *safe* place. She was going to be all right.

"Excuse me ma'am," said a friendly voice. "May I sit down beside you?"

Startled, she turned her head to see an overweight man with a balding head, a big grin on his flushed chubby face. He was wearing a blue pin-stripped sport coat, black tie, and gray slacks. She quickly deduced that he was a salesman.

"Mind if I sit down beside you?" he asked again, taking the seat next to her, not waiting for an answer. He looked harmless so she didn't object.

"These overseas flights can get to ya." he said, attempting to make conversation. "I'm a salesman for IBM and I've got to be in Amsterdam by tomorrow morning," he continued, loosening his tie from around his neck.

Rayemen didn't say anything. She just stared straight ahead. Amsterdam. *Yes, it's safe there. Got to get to Amsterdam.*

The salesman continued with his one-sided conversation talking about the weather, IBM, and everything under the sun.

He *was*, friendly. He *seemed*, safe. If she stuck with him, the strange man might not notice her. He wasn't expecting her to be with anyone, especially a nerdy salesman. She would be safe with him. Yes, *yes*, she must stay with him.

"Flight 201 to Amsterdam is now boarding at Gate 12," said the pleasant female voice over the public address system. "Please have your boarding passes ready."

"Mind if I get on with you?" asked Rayemen, turning to the salesman for the first time since he sat down beside her.

"Ma'am," he replied with a smile, "the pleasure's all mine."

Together they headed toward the gate, boarded the plane, and took their seats. Fortunately, they had seat assignments together. Amsterdam. It won't be long now. Amsterdam—it's safe there.

As the engines on the aircraft started, the salesman continued his chatter. He talked and talked. Then, his voice became lethargic. It sounded like a tape recording coming to a slow stop. Suddenly–*it stopped*. She turned to where he was seated beside her. He was bent over, eyes and mouth open; a silly smile still on his face. Startled, Rayemen looked around the interior of the aircraft. All the passengers were in the same position. Bent over in their seats, not moving. She looked toward the front of the cabin. There, standing in the middle of the aisle, was the strange man.

"WHY ME!?" she screamed hysterically, then everything went dark.

*****

As the bullet-shaped spacecraft soared through space, Rayemen lay unconscious on a metal table, covered to her head with a white sheet; her breathing labored, eyes closed.

"I thought we'd never get her back," said the first man.

"I know," began the second, "she's the best agent we've got. We almost lost her in that suicide bomber attack on her bus."

"Make a note," ordered the first man, "make sure that you change the dosage on the next agent."

"I will," said the second man, holding a glass vile full of a green liquid up to the light before speaking again. "This serum works perfectly. She actually thought she was from Earth. If only we had gotten to her before it started to wear off."

"I know," said the first man, shaking his head. "She became confused as to who she was. When the serum took effect, it blocked her memory of who she really was. When it started to wear off, her real self started to come back. Somehow, her mind became confused as to who she really is and who she was chemically programmed to be. We almost lost a good agent."

"Thankfully, we got her back in time," said the second man. "Thanks to those new real–life androids, and a little mind suggestion."

Back in Washington, a new agent is waking up in her modest apartment. Ready for a another day's work...*in the Pentagon.*

ZOONOSIS

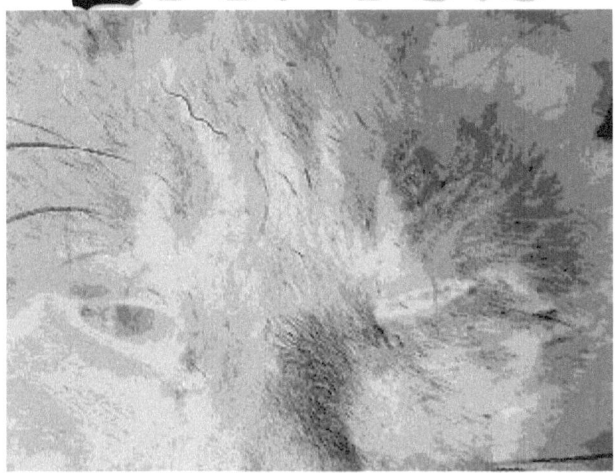

A faint light glows from the kitchen window of a dilapidated wood frame house. Four men are seated around a table, studying the blue prints of a building.

The first man points to an area that has been circled in red pencil. "That's were we'll meet," he says, looking at the other three. "Any questions?"

"Any security cameras?" asked the younger of the four.

"It's hard to be believe, but no," answers the first man, "we'll begin tonight at nine."

"Yes, nine," agrees another.

Randolph Laboratories is winding down its activities for the day. Employees of the chemical research lab are strolling out of the building, making their way to their vehicles parked in the employees' parking lot. Some are smiling and some have serious looks on their faces, still thinking about the days work they've left behind.

Inside the complex, clean-up crews are busy sweeping, mopping, and cleaning the various labs and offices. Some of the lab technicians are still finishing up last minute experiments, safely securing each in locked storage containers.

Lab 121 is still occupied. Outside the door, a man dressed in a blue jump suit is mopping the shiny tiled floor, moving his mop slowly from side to side.

Inside the lab, a technician has just finished securing his days work and prepares to exit the lab. As he walks out the door, his right hand flips the light switch, turning off the overhead florescent lights. Pulling the door shut, he types in a code into the electronic security panel mounted to the right of the door frame. A red light on the panel lights up; a small electronic beep can be heard, indicating to the technician that the lab is now secure. The lab technician smiles at the man with the mop, wishes him a good evening, and walks down the hallway. The man with the mop smiles back, but doesn't say a word. His attention is on the electronic panel.

As soon as the hallway is clear, the man with the mop goes to work. He pulls his cleaning supply cart over to the lab door. From the center of the cart, he pulls out a small leather case, and opens it. From it he retrieves a small screw driver and alligator clip wire. In lightening speed, he takes the front panel off the electronic lock and connects one end of the alligator clip wire to the exposed circuitry. The other end, he secures to a small electronic box in his hand. He pushes the button on the box. After two seconds of electronic sounds, the door to Lab

121 unlocks.

Quickly, the man disconnects the wire, throws it, and the box into the cart. Just as quickly, he secures the front panel back onto the electronic lock. He then opens the door and pushes the cart inside the lab, quietly closing the lab door behind him. From his pocket he pulls out a small flashlight and begins scanning the lab. After a few intense seconds, the small beam of light finally lands on its intended target; a small refrigerated case with a glass door. Inside are several color-coded glass vials. The man smiles. On the front of the case is a pad-lock. The man carefully, and expertly, picks the padlock.

Opening the case, he shines his flashlight into it, looking carefully at each vial. The man's smile now turns to a frown; his eyes narrow. Each vial is color-coded in three strips—red, blue and green and some green, yellow and blue. The color he is looking for is red, red and green, but it's not there. The nearest color code he can find is green, red and red.

He looks at his watch; it reads 11:20. He must rendezvous with the others in ten minutes. Red, red, and green. Maybe they labeled it backwards, or his contact got the coding mixed up. He grabs the green, red, and red vial and carefully puts it into a small muslin bag.

The intruder quickly exits the lab and heads down the hallway to the door with the red electric emergency exit sign mounted over the door frame. He has five minutes before the automatic alarm system activates, making it impossible to leave without setting it off.

"These Americans," he says to himself, "they're so careless. This is like taking candy from a baby."

Just outside the door, three figures dressed in dark clothing are crouched to the right of the door. The door opens and the intruder joins his comrades. Quickly they run away from the building, using the cover of the manicured shrubbery to conceal themselves. They run about twenty feet to the road and their car. One man opens the door, pulls a white flag out of the window, used to indicate the car was broken down. After the last man gets into the car, it starts, and they speed down the road.

The night is quiet. A doe is grazing peacefully, but cautiously; keeping a constant lookout for anything that may cause her harm. She points her nose straight up in the air, checking for strange scents. Behind her, a black and gray cat is playfully stalking. The cat knows it can't kill the deer, but it's something to do. If nothing else, it can run up and tag the deer on the leg. That would be a *victory!*

Suddenly, the deer catches the scent of the cat. Her ears perk up as she turns her head toward her backside. The cat freezes. In one quick movement the deer bolts forward. The cat jumps from its hiding place, in hot pursuit.

The vehicle speeds toward a steep grade. Inside, the men are laughing, and passing around a bottle of booze. They're celebrating their *own* victory. The driver is the only one who isn't drinking. He's concentrating on getting them safely to their destination, hoping he has the right vial.

"Have a drink Friend," says the man sitting in the front passenger seat, forcing the bottle in the drivers face.

"Get that away from me," says the driver, pushing the bottle away, "Are you trying to make me crash!?"

At that instant, the deer runs out in front of the vehicle. The driver swerves to the right to avoid it. The vehicle hits the ditch as the deer runs into the woods on the opposite side of the road. The vehicle flips several times, coming to rest on its top and bursting into flames. Then all is quiet, except for the sound of flames, and the crinkling noise of hot metal.

Three men inside he vehicle are dead. The driver lays half on the roadway, half in the ditch, his bloody head resting on the asphalt. He too, is dead. In the middle of the road lays the muslin bag containing the vial. Underneath it a liquid slowly trickles out.

The cat sits calmly on the side of the road observing the accident scene. Cautiously, it moves toward the man laying half in the road, half in the ditch. It sniffs the man, then sees the liquid moving on the asphalt road. As though in slow motion, the cat saunters to the muslin bag, and sniffs it. Its eyes catch the liquid movement, sniffs it, and then begins to lick it up. The cats drinking is interrupted by the sound of sirens. It perks up its head, listens, then runs back into the safety of the trees.

They call her Cat Lady, almost every town has one. Usually living in a rundown house on the outskirts of town. A middle–aged woman who has never been married, or her man has passed on, or ran off with a younger woman. To fill the void, she harbors cats. At present, Cat Lady has fifteen cats, of various breeds, under her care.

She starts her day by setting out five bowls of cat food, placing each at the bottom her back steps. Immediately cats seem to appear from nowhere, rubbing against her ankles and meowing a thank you, as they crouch down to eat their morning meal.

Cat Lady smiles and says good morning to each, bending over to scratch behind their ears. Slowly walking back up the old wooden stoop, she sits down on the top step. Picking up a cup of coffee she had placed on the porch, she begins to sip the freshly made brew.

Dressed in a flowered sun dress, wearing worn out tennis shoes with her hair in a ball, she looks like someone's granny watching over her grandchildren. Her whole body jiggles as she laughs at the small kittens running toward the bowls, tripping every few feet. When one of the cats begins to growl at another, wanting the food all to itself, she stamps her right foot. "Stop that Nero," she says, in a firm voice, "there's enough for everyone."

At the edge of the yard the black and gray cat peeks around a small tree. Cat Lady takes another sip of her coffee, and peers out into the yard. Her quick eye catches the movement of the black and gray.

"Well, what have we here?" she asks. "Who might you be?"

Slowly, Cat Lady gets up from her perch and walks toward the black and gray. The cat stands its ground, sensing no harm from her advance. She reaches down and picks up the black and gray. The cat gives in without a fight, purring contently.

"You're a friendly fellow." she says, stroking the back of the cats head. "I'll call you Mister."

She brings Mister to the foot of the back porch, and gently places him among the others. Immediately, Mister begins to eat, oblivious to the other felines.

"Now we are sixteen," says Cat Lady, as she climbs back up the stoop, laughing.

A detailed account of the accident was featured in the morning edition of the local newspaper. It mentioned the burglary at Randolph Laboratories, and the missing vial. The article said that the vial, recovered at the accident scene, contained a rare form of a zoonosis virus. The victims of the accident had been linked to the burglary, and since the vial had been recovered, there was no cause for alarm. Just in case, local authorities were asking citizens to keep an eye on their pets and wildlife, for any unusual behavior. They were to report this behavior to the local Animal Control office. Local and state law enforcement authorities were investigating the burglary, and as to why the thieves wanted the virus.

There was some speculation that it was part of a terrorist plot to inflict the virus on humans. Others ratiocinated that they were after the anthrax virus, the lab was housing. In any case, the vial had been recovered, and all the anthrax had been moved to another facility before the burglary, so there was no real need for concern.

Cat Lady picked up her morning paper from the end of her driveway. She took it inside, unrolled it, and began spreading the paper inside the five litter boxes. What she didn't use, she laid on a large stack of unread newspapers in the corner of her kitchen.

Mister looked at her with narrowing eyes. Another cat walking past him received a warning growl. Mister isn't feeling good. He is mad. Not at anyone, or anything in particular, he's just–*MAD*!

Inside the Animal Control complex, technicians and Animal Control Officers are busy with their morning duties. Cleaning cages, and checking animals the officers had brought in the night before, for disease or infections. Others are feeding the many unwanted dogs and cats whose futures are uncertain.

The ACO Chief watches as a technician grooms perspective cats and dogs going up for adoption. Contrary to the public's impression of Animal Control Officers, they love animals; just as much, if not more, than the average person. If it wasn't for irresponsible pet owners, their job would be a lot easier.

Next, he goes to the euthanizing room. This is where animals, no one wanted to adopt or had stayed their allotted time, are euthanized, in a specially made chamber.

"How many today?" the Chief asks, as a technician prepares the chamber.

"Ten today, sir," he replies.

"There should be a law that we could put down the owners, as well," says the Chief, as he walks out of the room, and heads toward his office.

The local Police Chief is waiting in the ACO Chief's office.

"Hey Bob," greets the Police Chief.

"Hi Tom," he replies, closing the door behind him. "What can I do for you?"

"You can tell me about this zoonosis, rabies, or whatever-you-call-it-virus, they found at the accident scene on Waverly Road yesterday," begins the Police Chief.

"Well, I really don't know much about it, except that its a rare virus, and far more contagious and swifter-acting then anything encountered before."

"Is there a vaccine or anecdote for it?"

"Not for this strain, not yet anyway. Besides it's been found and contained."

"I know," said the Police Chief, standing up. "I'm just taking precautions."

The Police Chief bids farewell to his old friend, leaving the ACO Chief to ponder over his last statement.

As the day wears on, Mister becomes more agitated. He doesn't want to be angry; it's something he can't control. Though he feels hungry, he refuses to eat or drink. He is *mad* at the food placed before him. He is *mad* at the drink given to him. As each minute passes, a hatred for the woman who has taken him in increases.

In his confused feline mind, he begins plotting ways to rid himself of those around him. They are aggravating to him. Useless beings that need to be elsewhere. If they don't leave, he will see to it that they do not function.

As Cat Lady walks back into the kitchen, she bends down to pick up her new found family member. Don't come near me, he warns with a growl. I don't like you. I hate you. I'll *kill* you. He is quick. He is deadly. He is MAD!

Covered in blood, Mister makes his way to his next victim. One by one, he kills, until all fifteen felines lay about the house and yard; covered in blood, lifeless. He should feel better, but he doesn't.

He has tasted blood and he likes it.

Mister slowly walks out of the house, into the yard, and down the street toward town; *daring* any living thing to get in his way.

Animal Control Officer Jones has just left the Complex on his way to pick up a trapped stray dog on Little Street. He had set the trap the night before. You *never* set a trap during the day. His Chief was adamant about that. Setting a trap in the day meant exposing a trapped animal to the hot sun. This could lead to heat stroke and death for the animal. Since they were limited with only five Animal Control Officers, they didn't have the time to check the traps often enough to set them during daylight hours, so he set them in the evening, checking them each morning. The property owner had called first thing that morning to let him know he had a dog in the trap.

As Jones drives his specially equipped animal control truck, he makes out the figure of a cat walking down the middle of the street. The cat appears to be drunk. Immediately, the officer recognizes that the cat is A.A.R. (animal control terminology for "Ain't Acting Right"). Jones pulls his truck over to the side of the road, about ten yards from the cat, and activates the amber strobe lights atop his truck.

Cautiously, he exits his truck, trying not to frighten the cat. From where the officer is standing, he can see that the cat isn't wearing the required rabies tag. Jones takes his heavy duty gloves out of the cab of the truck, and slides them on, one by one. He then walks to the side of the truck, opens a side door, and removes a specially made net.

The cat continues its slow walk toward him, staggering every few feet. The ACO is standing in the middle of the street, facing the cat. It looks like the two are ready for a showdown. It reminds Jones of a Clint Eastwood western. He, armed with his net, and the cat, armed with razor sharp claws and teeth.

Instinctively, Jones calls out to the cat, "*kitty, kitty*."

Something he regrets saying. If the cat is rabid, "*kitty, kitty*" will have no effect on the feline. He looks around to see if anyone saw, or heard him. A move the ACO should not have made. At that instant, Mister sees his chance for attack. In one swift movement, he runs and jumps toward Jones, landing on top of the man's head, claws digging into his skin.

Jones fights vigorously, grabbing the cat by its front legs, peeling it off his head. He throws the mad cat on the road, as blood drips down the front of his face. Mister attacks again, this time Jone's leg, biting and clawing voraciously. Blood begins oozing through Jones pants. The ACO screams in pain. He grabs the cat by the loose skin behind its neck, and tears it off his leg. The cat fights wildly as Jones throws it into the built-in holding cage on the back of the truck; slamming the door on his prisoner.

"Damned cat," curses Jones, "I'll personally put you down when we get back to the shelter, and it'll be a pleasure to chop off your head and have it sent off to be checked for rabies."

Grabbing a towel from the cab of the truck, Jones wipes what blood he can off the top of his head and face. He then puts the truck in gear, and speeds off toward the complex.

The receptionist buzzes the ACO Chief on the intercom. "Mr. Johnson is on the phone, sir." says the electronic voice, "he's wanting to know if an ACO is on the way to pick up the trapped dog on Little Street; what should I tell him?"

"Tell him he's own his way, replies the Chief, "and call Jones on the radio to see where he's at. He should have been there by now."

"Yes sir," she says. The conversation ends with an electronic click.

As Jones drives toward the Animal Control Complex, his vexation towards the cat increases. The more he thinks about it, the angrier he gets. It would indeed be a pleasure to put that animal down, and out of its misery—*and mine!*

"Base to ACO1," squelches the female voice on the truck's mobile radio.

"Leave me alone. Don't bother me. I'm on a mission. I've got to get back to the complex, and *take–care–of–this–cat*." says Jones, agitated, not talking into the microphone but to himself. The radio squelches again, with the same message from the female voice.

Jones isn't to be bothered with such trivial things, like answering his radio. He wants no part of talking to the female voice on the other end. As a matter of fact, he wants no part of talking to anyone. All he wants to do is *PUT–THAT–CAT–DOWN!*

The same message comes over the radio a third time. Jones jerks the microphone off its holder, and with one hand, rips the cord from the radio. He then beats it with the microphone until the red power light goes dark.

He doesn't like her calling him on the radio. That's all the little floozy is good for; calling him on the radio, or sitting at her desk doing nothing but answering the phone and looking pretty. He'd like to show her pretty. He'd like to show her how pretty messed up she'll be when he gets a hold of her.

The little slut. He'll show her. He'll make her pay for all the times she's called him on the radio, interrupting his lunch, just to go pick up a stupid animal in a trap. It's only an animal. What could it hurt to wait 'til he finished his lunch. If it died–it *died*. If she died–she *died*. What would it hurt, she's just an animal; a useless female animal, good for nothing but mating. That's it, he'll mate with her then kill her. Isn't that what the Black Widow spider does. Mate, then eat her lover. Yeah, you can call him a Black Widower spider. That's what he is. A deadly spider. He's like Spiderman, but deadly. Look out world, here comes the Black Widower in search of its prey.

"Heard from Jones?" asks the ACO Chief, walking up to the receptionist's desk.

"No sir," answers the pretty petite blond. "He's not answering his radio."

"Maybe he's out of the truck," says the Chief, thoughtfully. "Let me know the moment he calls in or returns."

The ACO Chief returns to his office, and closes the door.

It's dark inside–Mister doesn't like this. He doesn't like anything. He has to get out. Clawing doesn't work. Ramming his head against the cage door is fruitless. He tries sticking his paw out through the air holes to find the latch; but that doesn't work either. Mister has one thing on his mind; get out and–*destroy the man.*

It's hard to breath now. Mister is having trouble sitting up. Every time he tries to sit up he feels dizzy; he is weak. Should have eaten before he took care of Cat Lady and her feline family. Should have eaten–darkness is closing in. Mister doesn't feel good; he is sick and dying.

The animal control truck speeds down the driveway to the ACO complex, tires squealing as it makes its way through the curves. The truck rounds the back of the complex, and skids to a stop in front of the sally port. Jones steps out of the truck, mumbling to himself. He has a mad look on his face, and his bloodshot eyes make him look like a crazed man who hasn't slept in weeks. He has one thing on his mind; KILL THE CAT!

Opening up the cage door on the back of the truck, he reaches in to pull the cat out. It is lifeless. It doesn't move. Dead, stiff, gone to kitty heaven.

"Damn it," bellows Jones, "you little feline bastard. You robbed me the pleasure of taking your ass out."

Jones throws the lifeless body of Mister on the ground. His attention is now turned toward the sally port door where the receptionist is standing, wide eyed, hand over her mouth. In one quick cat-like movement, Jones leaps onto the loading dock; the receptionist screams.

The Police Chief pulls up in front of the Animal Control Complex, siren wailing, blue strobe lights flashing. He comes to an abrupt stop, in front of the main entrance, tires squealing. There are two marked patrol units and an unmarked also there, along with an EMS ambulance, and several rescue squad personnel. A fire truck is slowly coming down the drive, its Federal siren slowly winding down before silencing completely.

"What's the hold up?" asks the Chief in an agitated voice. He can't understand why everyone is standing around outside and not making an attempt to go in.

"Sir," begins a plain clothes officer, the only investigator on the force. "We didn't want to disturb anything until you got here."

The Chief doesn't realize that he has come to a crime scene. He had heard the EMS dispatched to the shelter over his car radio, but didn't hear what the actual call was. He had assumed that the ACO Chief had had a heart attack, or suffered some other medical problem. The two had been friends for years, and the only thing on his mind was getting to the complex to check on the condition of his friend.

He hadn't considered the fact that he might be walking into a crime scene. Once he heard the dispatch, the rest of the radio traffic had been tuned out.

"Chief," says the investigator, solemnly. "They're all dead."

The Chief's heart sinks. A warm numb feeling engulfs his entire body. He feels flushed and weak at the knees.

"What do you mean 'they're all dead'?" asks the Chief, trying to control his emotions.

"There's something you've got to see." says the investigator as he walks toward the entrance of the complex.

The Chief, not looking at anyone, follows; keeping his gaze on the front door. As the two walk into the lobby, everything appears normal, except for the missing receptionist. Dogs can be heard barking in the background, as they slowly walk through a heavy-metal door and into the holding area. The frightened canines begin to bark louder, some cowering in the back of their holding pens. Cats hiss, as the two men pass their cages.

Opening another door, they enter into a small room where the animals are euthanized. The Chief stops in his tracks, focusing his attention on the body lying beside the metal euthanizing chamber, its face frozen horrifically. It's the ACO officer, Jones. The investigator then reaches down and opens the door to the chamber. Inside, is the crumbled lifeless body of the receptionist.

"There's more," says the investigator, closing the chamber door.

Opening a door to his left, he motions for the Chief to follow.

This is the prep room, where animals suspected of rabies are prepared. The standard procedure is to cut off the heads of the infected animals and prepare the heads to be transported to the state facility, where they're tested for rabies. As the Chief enters the room, he almost becomes sick to his stomach. On the surgical table are four human heads. Their bodies lay lifeless on the floor around the table. The ACO Chief's head is also on the table; a wild expression on his face.

The Police Chief sits down in a metal folding chair, positioned against one of the walls, and puts his head in his hands.

"Call the state boys," he tells the investigator, without looking up. "There's more to this than we can imagine. We'll need all the help we can get."

A few hours later, the state authorities arrive in their unmarked vehicles. As the men and women in plain clothes get out of their cars, a black and gray cat sits on the hillside just east of the complex, licking blood off his paws.

Mister feels better now. Mister has his strength back. A short time ago he had awaken to a loud commotion coming from inside the strange building. Curious, he had walked into the building to see what was happening.

He saw the man who had fought him slamming people against the walls with super human strength. Tired of this, Mister decided to leave. He *is* feeling so much better now. Mister is hungry though, and thirsty. More thirsty than hungry. Mister needs to drink; not water, not milk—mister *needs* blood. He has a great thirst for blood. It has to be human blood though. Yes, he needs to taste human blood. That makes him feel better. Must find human blood.

Mister stands up, stretches, and slowly sashays toward town.

OVERLY PROTECTIVE

Mary awakens from her nightmare in a cold sweat. Her breathing is labored, and her heart feels as though it will burst out of her chest and fly away. Sitting up in bed, she holds her left hand over her chest, supporting herself with her right.

Dazed, but very much awake, she gets out of bed, and runs down the hallway to her four-year-old son's room. She cautiously opens the door and peeks in. The small child is laying on his back, eyes closed. Looking at his chest, she is relieved to see it moving up and down in a steady rhythm. Letting out a breath of air, she relaxes. He's breathing. He's alright. Quietly, she walks into the small child's room, bending over the sleeping angel and kisses him on the forehead.

Mary leaves the room as quietly as she entered it, and walks downstairs to the kitchen. Opening the refrigerator door she takes out the milk container and pours some of the white liquid into a pot; placing it on the stove. After turning up the burner, she sits down at the kitchen table and waits for the milk to warm. While waiting, she ponders over the nightmare she has just had; the only light provided by the moon shining through the kitchen window.

This isn't the first time she has been aroused from a deep sleep by this same nightmare. Ever since Johnny's birth, she has had the same nightmare, over and over again; sometimes twice a week, or she would go months without having it, but eventually she had it, the same terrifying nightmare. At first she thought the responsibility of raising a child on her own, and the fact that she is an unwed mother, was the cause for the nightmares.

At twenty-one she had gotten pregnant. When she told Johnny's natural father the news, he disappeared two weeks later, and hasn't been heard from since. She knew he was married, but he had told her he was going to leave his wife. That was two years ago. He did leave, but took his wife with him. An easy lay. That's all she was. How could she, with a college education, be deceived as she had been? She knew better, at least she thought she did. No, she was an easy lay—*very gullible*.

Now all she has is Johnny. At least something good came out of the doomed relationship. Johnny is her life; the only person she lives for and she takes every precaution to protect him. Some may say that she is overly protective, but they don't understand. That's why these recurring nightmares are so disturbing.

Getting up from the kitchen table she goes to the stove, pours the warm milk into a glass, and places the pot in the sink. Mary looks out the kitchen window, raising the glass of milk to her lips. The warm liquid soothes and calms her. Sitting back down at the kitchen table, she takes another drink and begins to recall the nightmare. It's always the same. The scenario may be different, but the outcome is always the same.

Mary finds herself on the same street. She doesn't know the name of it, but it's lined with trees on each side. It's a residential area, she knows that. There's always a lot of people gathered in an open clearing four or five to a group, talking. Johnny is close by her side.

Someone comes up to her and starts talking, then she hears the squeal of tires on pavement. A woman screams, as people begin running toward the road. She looks around for Johnny, but he can't be found. Panicked, she runs toward the road.

"Oh my God!" cries a woman.

Mary finally reaches the road, pushing her way through the crowd that has now gathered. When she breaks through, she sees a car. Under the car is Johnny. Then she wakes up, or at least she seems to wake up only to find herself in another nightmare.

Again, there are people standing around. This time they're all grouped inside someone's house. Again, she has Johnny by her side. Again, she begins to talk to someone. Again, the squeal of tires; the scream, and everyone rushing outside. Again, she runs to the road to find Johnny under a car. It's like having a nightmare within a nightmare, over and over again. What scares Mary is that it's always the same outcome; Johnny laying under a car. The only way she can tell reality from the nightmare is when she wakes up in her own bed.

Mary finishes off the last of the milk and walks over to the sink, washes out the glass and pot, setting them carefully in the drainer.

Running her hand through her long blond hair, she glances at the microwave clock. The green digital display shows 4:30 am. No need to go back to bed now. She's got to get up in an hour anyway and start getting ready for work. Reaching up, she opens the cabinet door and pulls out a can of coffee.

After dropping Johnny off at the daycare, Mary steers her beat up Honda Civic toward downtown and the Hannah Grille. Ever since she had Johnny, being a waitress is all Mary has been able to do. The hours are flexible enough and she can usually get off when she needs to. The pay isn't bad, plus the tips at Hannah's are better than other restaurants in the area.

As she drives, she thinks of what she could have been. In college she was studying to be a teacher, but when she got pregnant with Johnny her whole life changed. Without the financial support she needed from Johnny's natural father, she wasn't able to stay in school, so she quit; becoming a single working mom. Up to that point in her life things had been easy.

College was a breeze, and she thought she had found the love of her life. She was walking on air, when in reality she was walking on egg shells. She had already been working at the restaurant part-time while in college; making enough to support herself, and using her tip money she had saved over the years, to help pay for her schooling.

When Johnny came, the extra cost of raising a child was too much for her. She had to dip into her savings, which ran dry after a few months. Now she was working full-time at the restaurant, and working overtime when possible. It's not a life she enjoys, but it's the life she has made for herself and Johnny. If it *wasn't* for Johnny, she would be lost and lonely.

Three nights a week, she manages to go to night school working toward her teacher's certificate. She was lucky enough to find a baby sitter in her apartment complex who she trusts, and doesn't mind keeping Johnny at night. One day, she will eventually make something of herself; providing a better home for her, and her son. Tonight is her last night at school. If she passes her final exam, she will be done. She will finally have her teacher's certificate.

Two weeks later, Mary picks up Johnny and tosses him in the air playfully; he screams in sheer delight.

"I did it Johnny!" says Mary, excitedly. "I've passed. I'm a teacher."

Johnny continues his happy scream, as he and his mother tumble onto the couch.

"Everything is going to be alright," she says, catching her breath.

"We're going to make it. I'll get a teaching job, and we're going to make it."

Sitting on the couch, she puts Johnny on her knee. Mary looks at her son, smiling. He returns the smile and she hugs him.

"Let's go celebrate," she says. "Let's go get a milkshake."

"Yeah," squeals Johnny, running toward the front door.

The following Saturday, Mary and Johnny arrive at a classmates house. The yard is full of other classmate's, waiting on hot dogs and hamburgers cooking on the grill. As the two get out of the car, several classmates yell "congratulations!"; holding up beer bottles as a sort of salute. Johnny, instinctively, wants to run toward the swing set in the back yard, but Mary grabs him by the shirt.

"Stay close to me," she tells him, "you mustn't wander off."

With a disappointed look on his face, Johnny does as he is told. Holding his mothers hand, they make their way toward a group of people mingling in the front yard.

"Why don't you let the child go play on the swings?" asks an old man she doesn't recognize.

"I don't want him to get hurt," she replies, defensively.

"You know, you can't cheat fate," he says, with a sly smile, then turns and walks into the crowd.

Mary's heart sinks. The man scares her, and the elation she was felling dissolves. Spotting her instructor, she walks over and taps her on the shoulder.

"Why Mary, I'm so glad you made it," says the instructor.

"Who is that old man?" asks Mary, looking over the teacher's right shoulder.

Turning in the direction of Mary's gaze her instructor asks, "What old man?"

Straining her eyes, Mary searches the group of people, but doesn't see the man. Suddenly, she hears the squeal of tires–a woman screams. People run toward the road–Mary follows. It's not a dream. It's not a nightmare. She's awake. Where's Johnny!? My God, *where's Johnny*!?

Mary runs toward the road and pushes her way through the crowd of people. There's a car stopped in the middle of the road. Under the car...is *Johnny*. Mary freezes in her tracks. She can't move.

Then she sees the old man reach down, gently pulling Johnny out from under the vehicle. He carefully takes Johnny in his arms, and walks toward Mary. Tears are streaming down her face; she feels faint. The old man reaches her, and puts Johnny in her arms. Scared and crying, Johnny appears to be alright, except for a few cuts and bruises. Mary hugs Johnny, crying uncontrollably.

"You can't cheat fate," says the old man, putting his aged hand on her shoulder. "You must let happen, what must happen. Sometimes, it's not as bad as you may think."

The old man walks back into the crowd; the siren from an approaching ambulance can be heard in the distance. Mary turns to watch him.

In her mind, she hears the old man's voice again. "Let the child live," it begins, "let the child live out his destiny. You can't change it. It must be fulfilled."

There's a short pause as the old man turns to face her. "He has a long life to live," he says, not moving his mouth, "Now go live your life. Prosper and enjoy the time together you have been granted on this earth."

"Mommy, may I go to Billy's house to play?" asks Johnny, animatedly.

"Yes," replies his mom, "but be careful."

Mary pours herself a cup of coffee and sits down at her desk. Before her, lay a stack of test papers to be graded. She smiles as she picks up the first paper. The Rascals, "It's A Beautiful Morning", is playing on the radio. Mary smiles. Life is good.

Leave Us Alone

It's 2 AM as detective Tanya Black pulls onto the muddy Buddy Lee Road. She immediately turns off her headlights; relying on officers in rain coats, armed with flashlights, to direct her to the staging area. After parking her vehicle, she makes her way through the rain and mud to the Crisis Intervention Team command vehicle.

Tanya is team leader of C.I.T., the negotiators division of the county-wide S.W.A.T. Team. Ten minutes earlier, she had received a call-out page to a possible hostage situation. The deputy working that area had responded to a call of screams and shouting from an elderly woman's residence.

When the deputy arrived on the scene, he tried to make contact with the woman, but didn't get a response. It wasn't until he heard the slamming of a door and the scream of a woman, that he called his supervisor. The supervisor, after accessing the situation, called out the special teams.

There are four other negotiators already inside the specially equipped van, hooking up various pieces of communications equipment. A portable generator hums in the background, supplying power to the van.

Seeing that preparations are going smoothly, Tanya turns to

Officer Bart who has just walked up with pen and pad in hand.

"What have we got?" she asks.

Bart is the interviewer for the team. He has already talked with some of the neighbors, gathering as much information as he could, about the elderly woman.

"Well," he begins, looking down at his notes, "we've got an elderly female around eighty years of age. No one is sure of her real name, but they call her Miss Annie. She lives by herself, has no known living relatives, and is very much a recluse. She doesn't bother anyone, and no one bothers her."

"Does she have a lot of money?" Tanya inquires.

"From what the neighbors are telling me, no," replies Bart.

"Is that it?" asks Tanya.

"Y-e-a-h." replies Bart, hesitantly, turning over a page on his pad. "There is one other thing, she doesn't have a phone."

This isn't going to be easy. A negotiators job depends on a phone. It makes it easier to communicate with the subject. Without a phone, they'll have to use the throw phone, or a bullhorn.

"What about the suspect?" Tanya asks, lighting a cigarette.

"Haven't the slightest clue," replies Bart. "No one has made contact since the first deputy arrived on the scene."

"Then how do we know someone's in there with her?" questions Tanya, blowing a puff of cigarette smoke into the crisp night air.

"Because," begins Bart, sounding a little peeved, "several officers have seen what appears to be a man walking in front of the picture window. He appears to have something long in his hand, possibly a shotgun or rifle. It's really too dark to make out what he has."

At that moment, Major Reeves walks up to the negotiators command vehicle. "I've got everyone in position," he begins, looking directly at Tanya, "I want to use the throw phone as soon as possible, so have two of your people prepare to go down with us."

There are no questions, just action.

Two of the negotiators put on their vests and helmets. The lead man will carry the small canvas bag holding the phone; a second will carry the reel containing the phone line. The throw phone is used when a regular, or cell phone is not available, or practical. The phone is put in a padded canvas bag to protect it upon impact; since, as its name suggests, it is sometimes thrown. Yellow tape wrapped around the phone keeps the headset from jarring loose from its cradle. It's taken down by the negotiators to where the S.W.A.T. team is stationed. S.W.A.T. team members will then take the canvas bag to a door, or window, and throw it in. The tactical team had spotted an open front window earlier, and had decided to make the throw through it.

The two C.I.T. team members, assigned to carry the throw phone, also take a bullhorn with them, just in case the suspect refuses to use the throw phone. They'll stay behind the cover of the S.W.A.T. Team. Once the phone is inside, the negotiators can ring it from the command van. On top of the bag are instructions to open the bag, take the tape off the phone, and pick up the headset to answer. If everything goes well, a line of communication is started with the suspect, and the negotiations begin.

After several anxious minutes, the walkie talkie crackles, "Number 6 to command—the phone is in," says the voice on the other end.

"Command, advise C.I.T. to attempt to make contact," says the Major, over the walkie talkie.

Tanya picks up her walkie talkie and presses the transmit button, "C.I.T. copies," then turns to the others and says. "Let's get to work."

Alston, the C.I.T. member assigned to make contact, puts his headset on, and starts the tape recorder. Another member sits beside him, also with headphones; he is the coach. The coach can hear what is being said by both sides. He, or she, will write out questions for the negotiator to ask, or things to say to the person on the other end.

"Here goes," says Alston, pushing a red button on the console, activating the ringer on the throw phone. It took several tries before he finally heard the electronic click of the receiver being picked up on the other end.

"Hello," Alston begins. "Can you hear me?"

He could hear movement on the other end, but no one was speaking. "This is Alston with the Crisis Intervention Team, I'm here to help you," he continues.

"Leave us alone," says a low, husky voice.

"What's you're name?" asks Alston.

"Leave us alone," says the voice again; then the phone goes dead.

Alston makes several more calls, each time the voice on the other end says the same thing.

"Sounds like he's talking in a barrel," remarks Alston.

Finally, Tanya calls command on the radio, and tells them that the suspect is not cooperating. After a short pause, the radio squelches; the Major informs them that the S.W.A.T. team is ready to make entry. He orders the negotiators to continue making attempts to contact the suspect. As best they can tell, the elderly resident is not on the main floor. The silhouette of a man at a picture window is their target.

There is a tense moment of silence; then the radio crackles, as the command to "GO" is given.

As the officers, dressed in black and wearing ski masks, enter the house from the rear, they shout, "Sheriff's office," over and over again; strategically searching each room, as they make their way to the front. When they reach the front room, they make a quick scan with their helmet lights; only to find the room empty.

"Ground floor all clear," says the entry team leader, talking into his lapel microphone. "We're making our way upstairs."

The men in black, cautiously, advance up the staircase to the landing; searching each room, only to find them empty.

"Top floor is clear," says the entry team leader, speaking into his lapel microphone once again. "There's no one here."

It took an hour to completely search the residence. They found nothing; no blood, no body, no crime scene. The only indication that anyone had lived there was the immaculate condition of the house. By now it was daylight, and a search of the outside turned up nothing; no foot prints, blood or body.

As the Major surveys the scene, the negotiators enter to reclaim the throw phone.

"Excuse me, Major," says a negotiator, "you might want to look at this."

The Major turns to see the negotiator holding the canvas bag containing the throw phone. The negotiator has already unzipped the bag, and is holding it up so the Major can peer inside. The yellow tape is securely in place around the phone.

"Major, it hasn't been touched," states the negotiator.

Two months later, Tanya is doing research at a local newspaper, when she comes across an article that grabs her attention. It's a reprint of a story first published in 1910. The story reads of a young couple who lived at the end of Buddy Lee road. A family argument had occurred the following night; leaving the man of the house dead.

Upon further investigation by the sheriff, the husband had come home early from work to find his wife in the arms of another man. An argument between the three began, ending with the husband being mortally wounded with a blow to the head. This was done by the wife, using a fire place poker. The judge had ruled it self defense.

The husband's last words before dieing were, "I'll be back, someday, and I'll take you with me. When I do, no one will ever find a trace of you."

Tanya slowly looked up from the newspaper. "I'll be damned," she said aloud. "No wonder we couldn't find any foot prints, or any trace of forced entry."

She reaches into her pocket book to retrieve her cellphone, but stops before she finds it. "They'll never believe it," she says to herself, smiling.

Tanya closes her pocket book and walks out the door.

THE DEVIL'S NOTE

Running from his upstairs room, down the staircase, and toward the front door, Ray yells to his Mom, "Me and Larry are going to ride our bikes."

"You two be careful," Ray's Mom hollers from the kitchen, as the screen door slams shut. "Stay on the sidewalk, and don't ride too far. Supper will be ready shortly."

Ray runs down the front porch steps into the yard, where Larry is waiting with his bike. It is the summer of 1960. Parents do not worry about their children roaming the neighborhood unsupervised. You can pay less than a dollar admission to see a movie, and stay for more than one showing without getting kicked out. Corner drug stores still have soda fountains; candy bars are still a nickel. A productive and safe time, when the only thing that worries adults is the Cold War, and the threat of a nuclear holocaust. As for the children, it is a worry free life.

On this particular day Ray and Larry are on an adventure. As the two eight-year-old boys pedal their bikes down the sidewalk, their conversation focuses on....*the house*. The house in question is an old Victorian wood-framed structure that stands on the corner of North Main and West Miller Streets. Built sometime in the late 1800's, the house has stood the test of time. Though it's in need of painting, and some of the shutters are in need of repair, it is still a sturdy structure.

The yard is in desperate need of some sort of professional land-scaping, but is clean. Two large, overpowering untrimmed, oak trees stand majestically in the front yard. Due to this condition the neighbor-hood children have dubbed it the official *haunted house.*

The house is occupied by an elderly man who never seems to leave the residence and is rumored to have been a professional musician some years ago. His groceries are delivered to him every Thursday. That is the only time he can be seen, when he opens the back door to accept his delivery.

This is the boy's destination, riding their bikes to the overgrown field behind the residence to set up a stake out, and watch. They believe the old man is a vampire or some other creature of the night. Why else would he stay in the house all day?

Ray and Larry have surmised that, one day, something preter-natural will happen to the delivery boy. That's why they journey every Thursday to their hiding spot. Once there, they patiently sit and wait. If something grotesque is going to happen, they don't want to miss it.

The boys peek through the kudzu, as the grocery truck pulls into the back drive of the house. They watch in anticipation as the delivery boy opens the back door of the panel truck, taking out a box of groceries and walks up the wooden steps to the small screened in back porch. Putting the box under one arm, he knocks on the screen door. After a few seconds, the screen door opens; revealing the old man.

He is slender with long thin gray hair hanging precariously down to his shoulders. He has a short gray beard that comes to a point at his chin; giving him a devilish look. His clothing looks old, but clean. He's wearing a light brown woolen shirt and a dark brown sweater with leather elbow patches. His slacks are a light gray. Scuffed and worn black leather slippers cover his feet.

As the old man reaches out to take the box, he suddenly turns his head toward the boy's position. Ray and Larry freeze. The old man's gaze seems to peer through the kudzu, revealing their hiding place.

"He's seen us," whispers Ray, frantically.

"Let's get out of here!" says Larry, quickly crawling out of their lair.

The boy's crawl through the kudzu as fast as they can, trying to make as little noise as possible. When they reach the road, they jump onto their bikes and pedal as though their lives depended on it. Finally, they turn onto Church Street and head toward the safety of their homes.

Later that evening, having finished supper in their respective homes, the boys meet in Ray's backyard. They're spending the night in Ray's surplus Army pup tent. After reading all the latest comic books, playing ten games of cards and eating all the popcorn Ray's mom had prepared for them, their attention turns to the events of the day.

"I wonder what the old man is doing now?" asks Ray, as he pulls out two Snickers bars from his backpack, handing one to Larry.

"He's probably already changed into a bat and is flying around looking for someone to bite," says Larry jokingly, tearing the wrapper off his candy bar.

"Let's go see," suggests Ray.

"Are you crazy?" Larry exclaims, almost choking on the candy.

"C'mon on," says Ray, searching the tent for his flashlight. "We can peek into the window and see what he's up to; maybe he's got a girl with him."

That interested Larry. Stuffing the last of the candy bar in his mouth, he grabs his flashlight from under his pillow. Several minutes later the boys find themselves in front of the house.

Looking at it from the sidewalk, its sinister appearance gives them cold chills. The summer evening breeze causes the large oaks branches to sway back and forth, casting ghost like shadows on the house.

"I don't like this," says Larry, nervously. "It's too creepy."

"Look!" Ray pointed to a dimly lit second story window.

The silhouette of a man can be seen pacing back and forth, and then disappear from their view. Someone begins playing a piano. The music is melancholy, changing tempo several times; it's a strange piece. At times it crescendos to an almost deafening level; then suddenly drops so low you have to strain to hear it. The boys are hypnotized by its melody and then the music stops. The next sound they hear is the random banging of piano keys, followed by the sound of glass breaking.

"Let's get out of here," suggests Larry.

"No, wait," says Ray, "let's go up on the porch. He may start playing again."

"Are you crazy?" says Larry. "You heard him banging on the piano—*he's nuts!*"

Before Larry can finish his sentence Ray starts walking up to the porch. Larry shakes his head, mumbling to himself as he follows. The boys walk up the three wooden steps onto the porch. The old and worn boards squeak under their feet as they make their way to the front door. Ray attempts to peer into the house through the stained glass bordering each side of the door.

"Can you see anything?" Larry asks.

"No, it's too dark," Ray replies, "and this glass is uneven."

Suddenly, the door opens and they are face-to-face with the old man. He seems as startled to see them as they are him. In the moonlight, his gray shoulder length hair, gray beard, dark brown eyes, and pale white skin, give him a sinister look. He is still dressed in the brown woolen shirt, the sweater with leather elbow patches, gray slacks, and the black leather bedroom slippers; he has the smell of tobacco about him.

"What are you boys doing here on my front porch," he asks, looking intently from one to the other.

The boys are frozen, not able to move or talk. They want to run, but can't.

"Well," asks the old man again, more sternly, "I hope you weren't planning on ringing my door bell and running, because the door bell doesn't work."

Finally, Ray finds the courage to speak, "M-m-mom said you were once a great musician and, and I l-l-like music, and w-w-we wanted to hear you p-p-play, so w-w-we thought..."

"Thought you'd check out the weird old man; see if he was man or beast?" interrupts the old man.

Both boys look down, knowing that he is right and they are guilty.

In unison they say shamefully, "Yes sir."

"And your investigation has found what?" asks the old man, crossing his arms over his chest.

"We're sorry," says Ray, shyly, turning his gaze toward the old man. "It was wrong, but I do like music, and I liked what you were playing."

The old man's stern gaze relaxes and he begins to smile.

"Well, thank you for the compliment, but don't you two think it's a little late to be snooping around an old mans house?" he asks, speaking in a softer tone of voice.

"I guess so," says Ray, "its just that we were camping out in my backyard, and kinda got bored."

"Well, it's not that late," says the old man, looking at his pocket watch. "If you really want to hear me play, you can come in for a little bit, then home you go."

The boys follow him into the foyer. Contrary to its outside appearance, the interior is beautiful; furnished with expensive furniture (the type of furniture your mom never lets you touch, or sit on), and the hardwood floors look freshly polished. Off to the left of the foyer is what appears to be the living room; it too, is well furnished. A large Indian rug lay neatly in front of a granite fire-place. To the right of the foyer are two polished oak doors, closing off another room. Before them is a hallway that leads to other rooms, and a beautifully designed

Victorian staircase to the left. At the top of the stairs a light is coming out of a room. This is where the old man has been playing his piano.

"My music room is up here," says the man, as he begins walking up the staircase. "Oh, but I guess you two already know that."

Cautiously, the boys follow him up the steps and into the music room. Compared to the rest of the house this room is a mess. In the center is a black grand piano. There are stacks of sheet music every-where; scattered on the floor, chairs, tables, and an old Victorian style couch sits against the wall to the right of the piano. A antiquated rollback desk, against the opposite wall, is also covered with blank music sheets; books of various shapes and thickness, and a small lamp that sits on top of it. The only other light in the room is the piano lamp mounted over the piano keys. There is a small table to the right of the piano stool; here a coffee pot, cup, a block of cheddar cheese and ashtray sit. The walls are lined with book shelves that hold hundreds of books. Unlike the rest of the house, which smells clean, this room has the strong odor of tobacco, coffee, and old books.

"Have a seat," says the old man, holding his right arm out in a polite gesture, "if you can find a place to sit."

The boys manage to find enough room on the cluttered couch to sit. The old man sits on the piano stool behind the piano, and pours himself a cup of coffee.

"Care for a piece of cheese?" he asks.

"No thank you," answer the boys in unison.

"I would offer you something to drink but all I have is coffee," he says, breaking off a piece of cheese and putting it into his mouth.

"So you boys want to hear some music?"

"If you're busy we can go," says Larry, who is getting a little antsy about the whole situation.

"No, you can stay," says the old man with a smile. "Maybe you can help me solve a problem with this piece."

"How can *we* help you with it," inquires Ray, excited with the prospect of helping a real musician.

"I've been working on this piece for most of my adult life," begins the old man, "but when I get to the end of the third movement, I can't seem to find the right note."

"Can't you just change it to a chord instead of a note," queries Ray.

"NO!" exclaims the old man, angrily, "IT MUST BE A NOTE. ONE-SINGLE-NOTE!"

The old man closes his eyes and takes a deep breath before speaking. "I'm sorry, it's just that I've been working on this day and night for the past twenty years, and if I don't find the right note, I'll, well, I'll never be able to rest in peace."

The startled boys look at each other. Ray is beginning to think that Larry may be right'—the old man *is* nuts!

Slowly opening his eyes, the old man looks at the boys sadly.

"I'm going to tell you a story, but you must promise to keep it a secret."

"I will," agrees Ray.

"Me too," says Larry.

"I guess it wouldn't matter if you told anyone," says the old man as an afterthought, "they wouldn't believe you anyway."

He takes a sip of coffee, strikes a match on the side of the piano to light his cigar, then begins his tale. "I'm older than you may think; born in 1895. Both my mother and father were in show business. My father played the piano, and my mother sang. She had a such a beautiful voice. They made their living performing across the country working for various performing companies, so, naturally, I grew up around music. My homes were hotel rooms; my meals were taken in eatery's. The only education I received was from my parents and what I learned from show people.

"At the age of twelve, I was already playing the piano and performing with my parents. We weren't big stars, but we made a decent living. By the time I was sixteen, I had become an accomplished pianist. My parents had managed to save up enough money to get me into the Institute of Musical Art. They call it the Juilliard School of Music now. There, I was able to polish my craft and began writing my own compositions. Soon, I was giving my own concerts at school and won several music awards.

"After graduating, I performed with some of the best symphonic orchestra's in the world. For several years I played professionally; continuing to fine tune my craft and writing my own compositions. Though I enjoyed what I was doing, I was tiring of hotel rooms, restaurant food, and not getting the recognition I felt I deserved as a musician.

"One evening, following another successful concert, I was walking to my hotel room feeling sorry for myself. I deserved better! I felt
it should be *my* name up in lights—I should be the star. I wanted more
than just a hotel room. I wanted a large home, more money and fame.

"That night I had a dream, or what I thought it was a dream. A man
dressed in black came to my room. I don't recall going to the door to
let anyone in; he was just there, standing in front of me. The strange
thing about it, I *didn't* fear him. I felt as though he were an old friend
who had come to visit, but for the life of me, I can't remember how he
got into my room.

"He had a resonant voice and I became transfixed as he spoke. He
told me that he agreed with my feelings and that I *did* deserve better.
He said that he could make it happen. All I had to do was agree to sign
a simple contract. He then handed me a rolled up piece of parchment. I
unrolled it, and without going into great detail I'll tell you the gist of it.
It read that I would achieve fame and fortune, with the added benefit
of eternal life; and that, as long as I performed, I would be in the
spotlight, rich and famous.

"Skeptical, I asked what he meant by eternal life. He then pro-
ceeded to tell me that as long as I played a particular piece of music
everyday, I would have eternal life. If I failed to play it, then my life
would end, and my soul will be taken by the Devil. There was an out
to the contract, though. If I finished a particular composition and could
find the Devil's note, I would be free of the contract. Free to pass on,
and my soul would not be taken by him.

"I'm sorry to say, that it didn't take me long to decide. I was young and invincible then. I surmised I would have no problem finding the Devil's note when the time came; so I signed the contract. He than handed me the unfinished composition, and vanished.

"So, all these years, I've been trying to find the right note. I must play the Devils song daily in order to continue my life on this earth.

"You see, I am weary. I tired of the fame and fortune after several years, so I resided myself to this meager existence; living off my fortune, and spending all my time trying to find that, *damned* note."

The old man put his head in his hands. The boys look at each other in amazement; neither can speak.

After a few moments, the old man raises his head, smiles at the boys and says, "You probably think I'm crazy. I don't blame you if you do, but if one day you find that I am gone, you'll know that I finally found—the Devil's note."

After a brief moment of silence, the old man pulls out his pocket watch from his pants pocket. "It's getting late," he says, "you two had better get back home."

As the old man walks the two dumbfounded boys to the front door, Ray asks, "Can we come back sometime?"

"Sure you can," replied the old man in a lighter tone of voice, "but next time make it a decent hour."

After Ray thanked the old man for letting them visit, the two boys walked down the broken concrete walkway, towards the sidewalk and their bikes.

"Remember one thing," calls out the old man as an afterthought, "never make a pact with the Devil. It can never do you any good."

With that final comment, the old man closes the door. The boys then ride in silence, back to their tent.

Ray visited the old man on several occasions after that first meeting and enjoyed listening to the many compositions he had written. The old man even gave Ray free piano lessons.

One day, Ray knocked on the old man's door, but no one came. He went to the back door, but didn't get any response. He walked back around to the front door and gently opened it, announcing his presence as he walked in; still, no one answered.

"Hello," he calls out, "it's Ray, are you here?" All is quiet, except for the steady ticking of the fireplace mantle clock.

Ray slowly makes his way up the Victorian staircase and into the old man's music room, continuing to announce his presence. As he walks into the room, he can smell the strong odor of a cigar. Looking toward the table beside the piano stool, Ray sees the still smoldering cigar in the ash tray. Again Ray calls out, but there is no answer.

He walks over to the table and lightly touches the coffee pot, it's still hot. He touches the coffee cup, still full of coffee and warm. Then Ray turns his attention to the piano; old and worn sheet music is scattered on top of it.

Ray sits down on the piano stool and looks at the music before him. His hands, slowly and nervously, reach for the piano keys. Suddenly, he jerks them back. To his amazement, the notes begin to fade from the sheets of music. Ray takes his index finger and gently touches a corner of one of the pages.

As soon as he does, the sheet music disintegrates into a million micro-pieces. They begin swirling around the room, forming a small tornado, as a bright light appears from the center of the floor. The little tornado slowly rises into the air, hovering over the bright light for a couple of seconds, before being sucked down into it. The light then shrinks into a small beam, and retracts itself quickly into the floor. When the spectacle is over, calmness returns to the room.

Ray sits there for what seems an eternity, dumbfounded at what he has just witnessed. Finally, he gets up the nerve to move and run out of the room. He takes two steps at a time, as he runs down the staircase and out the front door.

Jumping on his bike, he pedals as fast as he can. When he gets home, he runs upstairs to the safety of his room. Once there, Ray sits on the edge of his bed wide-eyed and breathing heavily. Then, a peaceful calm comes over him and he smiles.

"He did it," he yells. "He found the Devil's note!"

Ray burst into a joyous laugh, dancing around the room, repeating over and over again, "He did it, he did it.....he found the Devil's note."

Twenty years later, Ray was able to buy the old house. He had it restored, except for one room—the music room. He left it as it was twenty years earlier.

Sometimes, late a night, you can ride by the house and see two silhouette's sitting behind the piano. If you're brave enough, you can sneak up onto the front porch and hear some of the eeriest music ever played.

A VISIT

It was a hot August night—one of those southern dog-day nights. I was home recovering from minor hernia surgery; the air conditioner hummed quietly in the background. I thanked God for the man who had invented it. Without it, my convalescing would have been very traumatic, so I spent my days of recuperation in the comfort of artificially cooled air, content to be in my favorite chair in the den.

After four days at home, not able to move around much due to the pain, I had settled into a routine of reading in the morning, watching TV in the afternoon, and sitting in front of the den window at night; armed with a pair of binoculars.

No, I'm not a peeping Tom; besides, I live in a remote area and my closest neighbor is a mile away. I *am* a fan of aviation and living two miles from the airport gives me the advantage of seeing many different types of aircraft. To me, watching the air traffic at night is a beautiful sight and very peaceful.

These convalescent days gave me the opportunity to try and spot a CL44 I had seen landing about a month ago. It was a beautiful sight. A four prop vintage Canadian cargo carrier; twice the size of a B-52 bomber. So, armed with my binoculars, a glass of milk, chips and dip, I began my nightly vigil in front of the den window.

There was little air traffic that night, except for an occasional small Cessna and some commuter flights. The sky was cloudless, full of stars, and a full moon.

Since it was such a beautiful night, I aimed my binoculars at the brightest star. The star I had chosen turned out to be more than I bargained for. The more I looked, the bigger and brighter it got. I had know idea that I was about to be paid a visit.

I was looking into the Eastern sky and as the star grew brighter, its color began to change from a bright white to a pale blue. Suddenly, it was gone. Taking the binoculars down, I looked to the sky with my naked eye and spotted it again, this time to the North. There was a flash, like a blue strobe light. Turning my attention to the ground, I expected to see a police car on the street behind my house, but the street was empty. I again looked into the night sky.

About a thousand feet up, I saw the blue light again. This time it was steady, not flashing; descending slowly and growing brighter. When the light was around a hundred feet from the ground, it turned its beam downward, making a blue circle of light in my backyard. I could now make out the outline of the source of the light. It was a ball-shaped metal object, about the size of a two car garage. I wanted to get up and fetch a camera or video recorder, but wasn't able to move. I tried with all my strength, but seemed to be paralyzed.

When the craft was ten feet from the ground, four metal legs emerged from the bottom; planting themselves firmly onto the ground. The craft was emitting a low humming sound, just loud enough to drown out the sound of the air conditioner. The craft settled securely on the ground. The blue light faded away and was replaced by a bright white light. This appeared out of the side of the craft. It was so bright

I had to close my eyes.

When I was able to open my eyes again, I could scarcely make out four humanoid figures walking down a metallic walkway protruding from the side of the craft were the light had been. They appeared to be around four feet tall, thin, with big teardrop shaped eyes; they wore tight gray jump suits. As they stepped onto the grassy lawn, they held the palm of their hands outwards and toward the ground radiating a beam of light. Then, they began walking around my backyard, using the beam of light like a flashlight. They appeared to be searching for something, unconcerned that I was sitting there, robbed of any movement watching them.

One of them did shine his light in my window and came up to it. He lowered his light, giving me a better look at his face. It was a peaceful face, smooth and waxen looking. Its mouth was small and seemed to be smiling. We stared at each other for at least thirty-seconds, then with a nod of his head, he turned, and continued his examination of my backyard.

They had been searching for about three minutes when the bright white light reappeared from the side of the craft. I closed my eyes, and when the light had vanished, so had the visitors. The small craft then began to rise slowly skyward, once again emitting a blue light from underneath. When it was out of sight, I was again able to move, but sat dumbfounded in my chair.

The next day I ventured out into my backyard looking for any evidence of their visit. At the spot where I had seen the craft land, I found what they must have been looking for. Ironically, one of the metal support legs had settled on top of it; pushing it into the ground. It was a small metal medallion, silver in color and engraved. A small chain was attached to it. The next day I packaged the medallion and sent it to a professor friend of mine who specializes in hieroglyphics.

Two months later, I received a package from my friend. Inside was the medallion and a note which read;

I have no idea what the metal is, but the inscription was simple to decipher. It's Egyptian, and reads, as I'm sure you know, for I believe this to be a practical joke of yours. "Scout Troop 901, Planet Anone." If you have no further use of it, I would like to have it as a deciphering exercise for my classes.

I keep the medallion in my desk drawer under lock and key. If they come back I'll return the medallion. Maybe, next time, just maybe, they'll stay longer.

Second Sector

(Star 9 System)

In the beginning, there were forty-five of us. A settlement of the United Colonies First Wave: scientists, researchers, medical, maintenance and security personnel.

The planet is located in the Second Sector of the Star 9 System. A "Class A" planet with over-sized vegetation and very little animal life. We had established a base camp about two and half miles from the ocean.

The first two years were uneventful, as we went about our daily studies of the planet. It was a peaceful existence, until two months ago when we were forced to live underground.

As head of security, I was making my usual nightly rounds to each of the security checkpoints. Afterward, I had planned to retire to my quarters for a nightcap and a good night's sleep.

When I reached Checkpoint 4, no one was to be found. I searched the area and then called on the two-way to security headquarters to see if they had heard from Checkpoint 4. The answer was "No". I then called to the other checkpoints and again received a negative. A search of the compound turned up nothing. A search party was formed and we ventured into the night in search of our missing officer.

The search party consisted of two units of ten security personnel. Each unit was given an area of two miles to cover, starting from

Checkpoint 4. We kept in radio contact at five minute intervals.

All was going well, until it was time for Unit 1 to check in. After thirty minutes of trying to raise them on the radio, five personnel from Unit 2 were dispatched to the last point Unit 1 had checked in. They would begin a second search as Unit 3; I stood by in the radio room.

Unit 3 had been out for about forty-five minutes, when the radio crackled. "This is Unit 3 leader, Roberts," said the electronic voice, breathlessly.

"Go ahead, Roberts," I answered.

"Sir, we've found something," he began. "Some sort of footprints, but they don't look human."

"You wanna clarify that, Roberts?" I asked, motioning the radio operator to turn on the recording equipment.

"They look like," he paused, "animal tracks." As Roberts talked, I could hear the others in his unit talking in the background.

"Wait a minute! Jones has found human tracks, too!" exclaimed Roberts. There was another short pause before the radio crackled again, "Sir, I think we've found the remains of Unit 2."

I lowered my head and squeezed the microphone button, "Can you tell what happened to them?"

"They've been torn apart sir," replied Roberts, his voice noticeably shaken. "Something has butchered them. Some have no bodies, just heads...God sir, this, this is...*terrible!*"

Then, in the background, I heard a scream and the radio went dead.

"Roberts, what the hell is going on?!" I shouted into the microphone, but didn't receive an answer.

"Roberts, Roberts!?" I pleaded into the microphone, "Answer me!"

Finally, the radio came alive again—the frantic voice of Roberts came through, "BUGS, SIR...DAMNED BIG...BUGS," he yelled, then the radio went dead...for good.

As I said, that was two months ago. Since then we have dug in, literally! Our only safe haven is this underground shelter.

During our excavations we have discovered, what I believe, is the cause for the giant bugs. A bunker was uncovered a week ago, providing us with the proof we needed; proof, that the planet had been occupied by...*humanoids*. In this bunker, we found antiquated metal file cabinets; each containing folders full of legal looking documents. There are also bunk beds, a kitchen and living area.

A bookcase full of old books was also discovered. Inside the bookcase I found one book that was particularly interesting. Bound in red leather and printed on the front in gold letters was:

HOW TO SURVIVE A NUCLEAR ATTACK
12th edition - United States Military Press

THE MARS LORDS
(THE BEGINNING)

*H*aving dinner at John's has always been a treat for me. He lives in a castle-like mansion, built of granite, that has been in his family for generations. As kids, we would spend hours playing in the many halls and rooms; so this visit, like many others, was a nostalgic trip for me.

As I walked into the dinning room, I noticed that John was more than pleased to see me—almost ecstatic. We usually sat in front of the big stone fireplace smoking cigars, sipping wine and talking, awaiting the butler's announcement that dinner was served. On this particular night, I seemed to be doing most of the talking. John just sat in his overstuffed leather chair, legs crossed, puffing on his cigar, with a silly grin on his face.

When we sat down to eat our meal of roast beef, cooked cabbage, potatoes and ale, I asked him what was bothering him. He smiled and urged me to finish my meal. Only after we had eaten would he tell me what was on his mind.

Finally, John laid down his fork, offered me another cigar and suggested we retire to the library. It was our custom to come to this oak paneled room, full of hundreds of books, for after-dinner conversation and a game of chess.

As soon as I had taken my usual chair, and John his, he began to tell me about his latest project; a project that would change our lives forever.

"Ray," began John, with his chin resting in his hands and a serious look on his face. "Have you ever wanted to go somewhere you knew was impossible to reach? That is, you thought was impossible?"

"Well, off hand I guess the North Pole. I've always wanted to meet Santa Claus; besides I've never seen real elves," I replied, jokingly.

"Very funny," said John, rolling his eyes. "What if I were to tell you that I have always wanted to go..." he paused, looking away from me for a second before completing his sentence, "...into outer space."

"Sounds great," I said, trying not to sound too discouraging. "But knowing you as I do, you don't have the patience to go through the necessary training. You'd be better off going with me to the North Pole."

John smiled, took another puff off his cigar, blowing the blue-gray smoke into the air, and said, "Ray, I have found a way."

"You've been reading H.G. Wells again, haven't you?" I stated sarcastically.

"Follow me," replied John, getting up from his chair.

As I followed, I began to wonder if my friend had finally lost his mind. It was understandable. John had been cooped up in this old mansion for years. Being the heir to a small fortune, he didn't have to work. He would rather spend his time tinkering in his wine cellar-which he had converted into a workshop-or reading. John, more or less, was an amateur inventor. Most of his inventions either didn't work, or turned out to be of no great use to anyone, except John. But at least it gave him something to do.

This, is where John was leading me. I had only been to it twice, that I recall. Once as a kid, when it was still used as a wine cellar, and again, when John had converted it to a workshop. He had shown it to me after its transformation several years ago.

As John opened the old wooden door, its hinges squeaked for want of oiling. He flipped a light switch to the "on" position, illuminating the stone stairs and walls.

"Be careful," John cautioned, "these steps can be slippery at times."

When we reached the bottom, John motioned for me to stop.

"Before we go any further, I must tell you that I've added a few new gadgets," he said, moving his hand over an electronic eye mounted in the wall. Suddenly, the stone wall before us began to slowly part in the middle revealing the workshop. It was alive with electronic activity. There were electronic devices of all shapes and sizes; computers and other gadgets that twinkled with colored lights.

Large flat screen monitors lined the walls of the rectangular shaped room, displaying rotating geometric shapes, maps of the solar system, and computer generated models of space craft. At the far end of the room was a huge metal door, outlined with flashing red lights.

The only part of the room that resembled the old wine cellar was the stone ceiling. The walls and floor were made of some sort of shiny metal. John, boastfully, told me that it was a new type of aluminum he had invented. Strong enough to support tons of weight and durable enough to withstand heat and fire. Even the intense heat experienced by a space craft reentering the Earths atmosphere.

John gave me a quick tour of the workshop, explaining what each piece of equipment did. I listened, but I must confess, I didn't understand a word he was saying, so I just nodded. When we had walked the length of the room, we found ourselves in front of the huge metal door.

"Well," John said, rubbing his hands together. "What do you think?"

"Impressive," I answered, "but I really don't understand what it's for."

"This," said John, waving his right hand in front of another electronic eye. There was a loud metal clank and the huge metal door began to rumble and part in the middle. A bright white light shot its beam through the crack. I began to hear a low humming sound from behind the doors. The more the doors parted the louder the hum and the brighter the light became.

When the doors finally retracted to their resting place, I hesitantly followed John into the white light. As we entered, the light dimmed and the humming subsided. To my amazement, I was staring at what appeared to be a flying saucer.

We were standing in a room as big as an airplane hanger. The craft I was looking at was about five hundred feet in diameter and sixty feet in height, supported by four metal legs. It was made of the same aluminum material John had invented. There were several small port windows around the upper part of the saucer shaped craft. We entered the ship through a side door which was invisible to the naked eye when closed. This, John opened by placing his hand on a small black circle on the side of the craft.

Inside, the walls were lined with flashing lights, different types of electronic controls and computers. In the center was a metal control panel and two futuristic-looking chairs behind it, both securely bolted to the floor. There was a kitchen area to the right, complete with a microwave oven and a custom-made refrigeration unit. A permanently mounted oval table and six chairs sat in the middle of this area. To the left of the control center was a combination living and sleeping area which housed two well-cushioned chairs and two slide-away beds.

There were two levels. The upper level, which we were in, and a lower level which housed the propulsion system and several cargo bins. John said the propulsion system was some type of anti-matter electromagnetic device, or something like that. This was another of John's creations.

"Impressive!" I said, looking around in awe, "But can it fly?"

John looked at me with a grin and motioned for me to take a seat behind the control panel; he took the chair to my left. John then instructed me to buckle up the safety harness as he began pushing buttons and flipping switches, causing the craft to vibrate and hum.

As I looked out of the overhead view window, I could see the ceiling open up, revealing an evening sky full of stars. When the ceiling door had opened completely, the humming sound from the propulsion system grew louder.

"Ready to ride?" asked John, still pushing buttons and flipping switches.

"As I'll ever be," I replied, wondering what the hell I was doing.

Slowly, the ship began to rise into the night.

"What do you think of my little toy?" asked John, smiling from ear to ear.

"This is great!" I answered, excitedly. "I really didn't think you could pull off something like this."

John took us up about two thousand feet, and put the craft in hover mode. He sat back in his seat looking at the view screen; lost in deep thought. Suddenly, sitting straight up, he leaned over the control panel and again began his meticulous pushing of buttons and flipping switches.

"I think it's time to see what this baby can really do," he said, still concentrating on the control panel before him.

"Fine," I said. "You're driving."

John typed something into the ships computer and instantly we were off again. We were traveling a lot faster now, heading toward the stars, when a bright flash of light came out of nowhere, heating the interior of the craft like an oven. Just as quickly, it was over and everything seemed to be back to normal, or so I thought.

The next word out of John's mouth was, "Oops!"

"What do you mean by—*Oops*?" I asked, sounding a little worried.

"I can't seem to stop," he said, frantically pushing buttons, flipping switches and typing commands into the crafts computer.

I suddenly had a flashback to a time when John had experimented in developing a toy flying saucer. That too failed. He couldn't get it to stop either. It eventually crashed into a pond and sunk to the bottom, never to be seen again. Funny how the mind seems to bring up unpleasant thoughts at times like this.

I turned my attention to the view screen, hoping to block any more past memories of John's failed inventions, when I noticed that the stars looked like long streaks of light.

"What's causing that?" I asked John.

"We seem to be traveling faster than the speed of light, I think." John answered, as he continued his vigorous pushing, flipping and typing. "Somehow the ships magnetic field and the Earths have combined; causing some type of sling shot effect. We've literally been shot into space." He paused long enough to run his hands through his hair before continuing. "And it looks like we're heading straight for Mars."

I closed my eyes and said a prayer.

As Mars came into view, John had finally gained some control over the craft and was able to decrease our speed. From our vantage point in space the planet's surface appeared to be an eerie red. Thoughts of hostile Martians, with grotesque body's and an appetite for humans, raced through my mind.

"I've regained enough control to hopefully make a safe landing," said John, "but it may be rough."

Rough it was! We hit the red planets surface hard, bounced, and hit again and again, until our craft finally rested inside a huge crater.

"Are you alright?" asked John, after the craft stabilized.

"Yeah, a little shaken but at least in one piece." I replied.

"We appear to have sustained some damage," said John, slowly surveying the interior of the craft. Sparks were flying from various pieces of equipment, giving off small puffs of smoke. "We might be here a while."

I suddenly felt sick, closed my eyes and passed out.

When I regained consciousness, I found I was still fastened in my chair; a wet rag on my forehead. John was below rummaging through the crafts storage units pulling out articles of clothing, food packets and oxygen tanks.

"Awake?" John inquired, when he came topside carrying two plastic crates. He precariously dropped them on the floor.

"Yeah," I answered, still trying to come to my senses.

"Here, drink this." John handed me a soda he had retrieved from the refrigerator. "It'll settle your stomach. You appear to have gotten a bad case of sea sickness."

I unbuckled myself from the seat, took the soda and opened it, drinking half its contents in one gulp and then belched.

"What's next?" I asked, leaning my head back on the headrest.

"Well," John began, scratching the side of his face, "we need to go outside and see what kind of mess we're actually in."

"Outside?!," I said startled, almost spilling my drink.

"Yep, put this on," he said, handing me a flimsy looking silver jump suit and a briefcase size plastic box he had pulled out from one of the crates.

"What's this?" I asked.

"A couple more of my inventions," said John, taking another suit and box out of the crate for himself. "It's a light weight space suit, completely insulated and more durable than what NASA has, and a portable oxygen generator, good for twenty-four hours."

I took the suit, and box, wondering if these inventions would work. As I dressed, it suddenly dawned on me that we were about to be the first men on Mars. Too bad no one may ever know about it.

Once outside, I was able to get a better look at he planet's surface. It really was *red*. There were rocks and craters of various sizes and shapes scattered about. If there was life on this planet, it surely didn't live on the surface.

We walked around our craft, looking for any sign of structural damage; fortunately, there was none. The only apparent problem we faced was that the craft was partially buried in the red Martian earth and we didn't have the proper tools to dig ourselves out with. All hope of leaving the red planet began to fade.

"Well, that's that," said John, exasperated, "we might as well explore this crater we're in while I try and figure a way of getting us out of here."

The crater was about the size of a football field. Its walls were around fifty feet high and seventy feet thick. After we had walked about ten yards, I noticed what looked like the entrance to a cave in the crater wall. After pointing it out to John, we decided to explore it.

Reaching our destination, we turned on our helmet's exterior lights and walked in. We immediately found ourselves walking down a steady decline. At first, the tunnel walls and floor were dry and rough, but the further we descended, they became damp and smooth. About two hundred feet down, the tunnel ended, and we found ourselves in a large cavern. Light from some unknown source was filtering down from above, illuminating the cavern with a eerie red glow. There was a small pond to the left. The steady dripping of water could be heard echoing throughout the cavern. I looked for another exit but couldn't find one so I joined John who was already investigating the pond.

"Look at this," said John, pointing to the center of the pond.

In the middle of the pond there was a red plant growing under the water.

"What are they?" I asked, leaning over the edge to get a better view. "They look weird."

"You know what this means," said John, ignoring my question. "There's life on Mars, even if it is only vegetation."

John wanted to take some of the plants back for a closer look so we spent the next five minutes harvesting as much of the red plant we could carry, then headed back through the tunnel, and to our space-craft.

Once inside, we shed ourselves of the spacesuits and took the plants to the oval table for a better look. They were dark red in color with a smooth texture. Their roots were long, about twelve inches, which grew out of a golf ball size bulb at the base of the plant. John speculated that these roots gave them the ability to anchor themselves to the Martian rocks at the bottom of the pond. Pods, two inches in width at the base that gradually decreased to a point at the top, were growing from the bulbs. There were four to six pods to each plant. Each plant weighed from one to two pounds.

John cut one of the pods open revealing a meaty-like substance. It looked like a link sausage about an inch long and half an inch in diameter. It was a lighter red then the pod, almost pink; the aroma was sweet.

"They look good enough to eat," said John, after plucking one from the pod and holding it up to the light.

"Wonder if there are anymore?" I asked, picking up one of the plants.

Probably underground," began John. "I would venture to say, there is some type of underground stream, lake, or even ocean below the surface."

Then, John did the unthinkable. He picked up a salt shaker, sprinkled some on one of the sausages and took a bite out of it. "Not bad, here try one," he said, handing me a freshly picked Martian sausage.

Reluctantly I took it, salted it, and bit into it. It tasted like a combination of sausage and ground beef. I noticed that as I ate my whole body felt revitalized. I felt younger, clear headed, and every one of my senses seemed to perk up—I felt *great*!

"This stuff's *fantastic*," I said. "It's like eating a bottle of vitamins."

"Well," said John, in between bites, "we at least have solved our food supply problem."

John finished his meal of Martian sausage first and opened a soda, downing most of its contents, burped and said, "Now, if I only had a cigar."

No sooner had he gotten the words out of his mouth, when a cigar materialized on the table. Needless to say, we were both startled at the manifestation.

"Did you see that!" John exclaimed, now standing, eyes wide and mouth open.

"I see it but I don't believe it." I said, leaning over to get a better look. "Is it real?"

Picking up the cigar, John put it to his nose. "It smells real." He then bit off the end, spit out the excess, and wet it with his tongue. "Tastes real." Putting it in his mouth, he then produced a lighter from his pocket and lit the cigar. "By God, it is real!" he said, blowing out a puff of smoke. "It tastes Cuban."

"But how?" I asked, not expecting an answer.

John placed the cigar in a metal tray on the table, and for several seconds we just looked at the cigar, the red plant, and then slowly, we looked at each other and smiled.

During the next several weeks we experimented with our new

found discovery. We stewed it, fried it, sauteed it, and made soup out of it. We also discovered that the plants strange powers included being able to breath the thin Martian atmosphere. Our strength increased ten-fold, along with our vision and hearing. By Earth's standards, we were supermen. The effects of the plant depended on how much of it we consumed. For example, a mouthful was good for two or three hours, a plateful would last twenty-four hours. The only side-effect was that our eyes, hair, and skin turned red ten minutes after we had eaten the plant. Fortunately, as the effects of the plant wore off, we regained our original complexion.

With the help of our new found powers, we were able to physically push and pull our craft out of the Martian soil. Soon after repairing the damaged electronic components inside the ship, we were ready for our return trip home.

On the day of our departure, we filled up two large storage bins of the red plant. John wanted to try and cultivate our discovery back on Earth.

Our journey home was uneventful and we soon found ourselves back in John's library, discussing the the future of our find. John and I talked of the possibility of marketing the plant but ruled out that idea for fear of it getting into the wrong hands. After hours of discussion, several cigars and glasses of wine, we came up with the answer.

We would keep the secret of the plant to ourselves; in return, we would use its powers to benefit mankind. In other words, we were going to be *superheros.* The powers would only be used when all legal means had been exhausted. Realizing that when we used these Martian powers our appearance would attract a lot of attention I, reluctantly, agreed to wearing a superheros costume.

Since one of John's ancestors, from jolly old England, had been a Lord, we became the Mars Lords. The costumes were red with black trim. They had a black circle on the chest, with the letters M. L. in the middle, they were white in color. John wanted to have a black cape but thank God I talked him out of that.

When we put the costumes on for the first time, we looked like a cross between Spiderman and Superman. As we looked at ourselves in a mirror, I couldn't believe that two middle aged men, dressed in superhero costumes, were about to take on the criminal element of the world.

Over the next several months we continued to discover new powers. Other than being able to make objects materialize, just by thinking about them, we also could transport ourselves from one location to another. This was done by concentrating on a location, and within seconds we were there. We were well protected too! John found this out by accident during one of our experimental escapades when he fell off a roof onto the pointy end of a wrought iron fence post, bending it downwards.

As things go, we didn't discover the art of flying until after *I* accidentally fell off a roof. The ability to send a debilitating bolt of electricity also came by accident when I tried to throw some dirty laundry into the hamper, setting it, and the laundry on fire. All we had to do was point our index finger at an object, and *zap*.

Our hearing, vision, and physical strength were increased drastically, as well as our sense of smell. The latter proved to be a hindrance at times. We had never known how many foul odors there were in the world.

John was able to cultivate the Martian plant in a specially built green house, guaranteeing an endless supply of the super food. Now that we had our super powers, the next step was to use them—and use them we did.

We fought petty thieves, gangs, mobsters, and every criminal element you could think of. This, naturally brought attention to us. It wasn't long before newspapers, and other media sources around the world, were reporting on the mysterious duo called—*The Mars Lords*.

Though covert government organizations have attempted to find out who we are, and where we live, we continue to successfully keep our identity a secret. Not wanting to be committed to any one government, we decided to remain neutral; answering to no one, but ourselves.

The hardest part is not being able to tell anyone who we really are. You have a secret you're dying to tell, but you know you can't.

So, there you have it. This is the story of how *The Mars Lords* came to be. I am putting this writing in a safe deposit box to be opened and read, only after John and I have passed from this earth. Until then, we will continue to do what we can with the powers instilled upon us by the Martian plant; to protect and serve the people of this upside down world of ours. The powers of the Martian plant have been gifted to us. A gift we have sworn to keep secret.

We returned to Mars only once after our initial visit, and that was to close the cave entrance that led us to the Martian plant. For now, our discovery will be safe from getting into the wrong hands. The exact location of the crater and the cave, will never be revealed. That will die with us.

John has just summoned me. We must go now and do our duty, for we are *The Mars Lords*.

SWEET DREAMS